THE TWO HEROINES OF
PLUMPLINGTON

THE TWO HEROINES OF PLUMPLINGTON

By

ANTHONY TROLLOPE

AUTHOR OF "CHRISTMAS AT THOMPSON HALL", "THE WARDEN", & THE PALLISER NOVELS, ETC.

Caledonia Press

©1980 by Caledonia Press

Published as a volume in the Harting
Grange Library Series

ISBN 0-932282-48-2 (softcover)
ISBN 0-932282-49-0 (hardcover library binding)

LC Card Catalog Number 80-68022

Printed in the United States of America

Caledonia Press
P.O. Box 245
Racine, Wisconsin
53401 U.S.A.

123456789

Preface

"A Christmas story," Trollope said in his *Autobiography*, "should be the ebullition of some mind anxious to instil others with a desire for Christmas religious thought, or Christmas festivities, — or, better still, with Christmas charity."

Unfortunately, he says, many times such stories have "no real savor of Christmas about them," but are instead tenuously "fixed to Christmas like children's toys to a Christmas tree." The writing of *these* stories, Trollope admits can be distasteful, even funereal, since they are shams of the real thing, made up to be precisely what they aren't.

If this criticism is true sometimes, as we all know it is, certainly is does *not* apply to Trollope's *The Two Heroines of Plumplington*. This story cannot be read without sensing immediately Trollope's own excitement and enthusiasm, — his ebullition! to use his own word. Why?

Partly of course because the story *is* one of Christmas expectation, festivity and charity. These emotions embue all of Trollope's best writing, from *The Warden* with its portrait of the gentle Mr. Harding, to *Pineas Finn* and the silent loving Plantagenet Pallister.

But there is a more mundane reason, ironic as that may sound, for Trollope's high spirits with *The Two Heroines of Plumplington*. In writing this story he is back home among the roads and ridings, the beeches and pillar-boxes of Barsetshire, that imaginary English county he began exploring thirty years earlier. How he loved that county — divided into East and West Barsetshire, where, among others, the towns and villages of Barchester, Silverbridge, Hogglestock, Framley and Greshambury are located.

For twelve years, from 1855 to 1867, Trollope wrote six novels, chronicalling the life of Barsetshire. In a sense, which will be qualified in a minute, he ended all the Barsetshire novels when he wrote *The Last Chronicle of Barset*. In the final paragraph of that novel he wrote: "...to me Barset has been a real county, and its city a real city, and the spires and towers have been before my eyes, and the voices of the people are known to my ears, and the pavement of the city way are familiar to my footsteps. To them all I now say farewell."

True, Trollope said his sad farewell to Barsetshire in 1867, in *The Last Chronicle*, but then what did he do in his next novel, *The Claverings*, but mention some of the Barsetshire people. What's more, even before 1867, he had begun a new novel series, the Political or Palliser novels, in which some of the people of Barset are central personages — the Duke of Omnium, for example, and his nephew and heir Plantagenet Palliser, from whom the series takes its name.

It was difficult for Trollope to exile himself from Barset-shire. He loved it and its people too well. He left it reluctant-ly, and, as I have said, not entirely, though it was a necessary thing for him as a writer to do.

Yet how tempting it must have been for Trollope to return to Barset's familiar streets and towers.

In the last year of his life, in 1882, he made just that journey. He was sixty-seven. By now he had authored over sixty books, he had edited a quarterly journal, he had writ-ten countless reviews and essays for magazines and newspapers. He had traveled the extent of the British Com-monwealth, from Jamaica to New Zealand — and he had been to Iceland and Egypt, America and Panama. But in his last year he returned to his little green county, to the Barset-shire he created, peopled and loved.

It is no wonder that the story of this last visit is so em-bullient. *The Two Heroines of Plumplington* could not be otherwise.

"All the world may not know," Trollope announces at the beginning of this story, "that Plumplington is the second town of Barsetshire, and though it sends no member to Parliament, as does Silverbridge, it has a population of 20,000 souls, and three separate banks."

Plumplington. Trollope doesn't locate it precisely for us, but it must be in East Barsetshire, south of Barchester, somewhere near Plumstead Episcopi (residence of the Veneral Dr. Theophilus Grantley, archdeacon of the cathedral and rector of the Episcopi) and Plumstead proper (residence of Dr. Fillgrave, Dr. Thorne's principal rival among the Barsetshire medical profession, who is mentioned in the chronicles known as *Barchester Towers, Dr. Thorne,* and *The Last Chronicle of Barset*).

Trollope wrote *The Two Heroines* for the Christmas number of *Good Words,* but three weeks before the story appeared, on December the 6th, 1882, he died of a stroke.

In all, the story is typically Trollope, from the two vexed but resourceful girls in love, to Trollope's assurance we would immediately recognize the import of Plumplington by the fact of its three separate banks. And it fulfills his requirement for a proper Christmas story, since it cannot but instil you with Christmas expectation, charity and festivity.

John Kingsley Shannon

THE TWO HEROINES OF
PLUMPLINGTON

CHAPTER ONE

THE TWO GIRLS

IN the little town of Plumplington last year, just
about this time of the year,–it was in November,–
the ladies and gentlemen forming the Plumplington
Society were much exercised as to the affairs of two
young ladies. They were both the only daughters of
two elderly gentlemen, well known and greatly res-
pected in Plumplington. All the world may not know
that Plumplington is the second town in Barsetshire,
and though it sends no member to Parliament, as does
Silverbridge, it has a population of over 20,000 souls,
and three separate banks. Of one of these Mr. Greenmantle is the manager, and is reputed to have shares
in the bank. At any rate he is known to be a warm
man. His daughter Emily is supposed to be the heiress
of all he possesses, and has been regarded as a fitting
match by many of the sons of the country gentlemen
around. It was rumoured a short time since that young
Harry Gresham was likely to ask her hand in marriage,
and Mr. Greenmantle was supposed at the time to
have been very willing to entertain the idea. Whether
Mr. Gresham has ever asked or not, Emily Greenmantle did not incline her ear that way, and it came
out while the affair was being discussed in Plumplington circles that the young lady much preferred one
Mr. Philip Hughes. Now Philip Hughes was a very
promising young man, but was at the time no more

than a cashier in her father's bank. It become known at once that Mr. Greenmantle was very angry. Mr. Greenmantle was a man who carried himself with a dignified and handsome demeanour, but he was one of whom those who knew him used to declare that it would be found very difficult to turn him from his purpose. It might not be possible that he should succeed with Harry Gresham, but it was considered out of the question that he should give his girl and his money to such a man as Philip Hughes.

The other of these elderly gentlemen is Mr. Hickory Peppercorn. It cannot be said that Mr. Hickory Peppercorn had ever been put on a par with Mr. Greenmantle. No one could suppose that Mr. Peppercorn had ever sat down to dinner in company with Mr. and Miss Greenmantle. Neither did Mr. or Miss Peppercorn expect to be asked on the festive occasion of one of Mr. Greenmantle's dinners. But Miss Peppercorn was not unfrequently made welcome to Miss Greenmantle's five o'clock tea-table; and in many of the affairs of the town the two young ladies were seen associated together. They were both very active in the schools, and stood nearly equal in the good graces of old Dr. Freeborn. There was, perhaps, a little jealousy on this account in the bosom of Mr. Greenmantle, who was pervaded perhaps by an idea that Dr. Freeborn thought too much of himself. There never was a quarrel, as Mr. Greenmantle was a good churchman; but there was a jealousy. Mr. Greenmantle's family sank into insignificance if you looked beyond his grandfather; but

Dr. Freeborn could talk glibly of his ancestors in the time of Charles I. And it certainly was the fact that Dr. Freeborn would speak of the two young ladies in one and the same breath.

Now Mr. Hickory Peppercorn was in truth nearly as warm a man as his neighbour, and he was one who was specially proud of being warm. He was a foreman, – or rather more than foreman, – a kind of top sawyer in the brewery establishment of Messrs. Du Boung and Co., a firm which has an establishment also in the town of Silverbridge. His position in the world may be described by declaring that he always wears a dark coloured tweed coat and trousers, and a chimney-pot hat. It is almost impossible to say too much that is good of Mr. Peppercorn. His one great fault has been already designated. He was and still is very fond of his money. He does not talk much about it; but it is to be feared that it dwells too constantly on his mind. As a servant to the firm he is honesty and constancy itself. He is a man of such a nature that by means of his very presence all the partners can be allowed to go to bed if they wish it. And there is not a man in the establishment who does not know him to be good and true. He understands all the systems of brewing, and his very existence in the brewery is a proof that Messrs. Du Boung and Co. are prosperous.

He has one daughter, Polly, to whom he is so thoroughly devoted that all the other girls in Plumplington envy her. If anything is to be done Polly is asked to go to her father, and if Polly does go to her father the thing is done. As far as money is concerned it is not known that Mr. Peppercorn ever refused Polly anything. It is the pride of his heart that Polly shall be, at any rate, as well dressed as Emily Greenmantle. In truth nearly double as much is spent on her clothes, all of which Polly accepts without a word to show her pride. Her father does not say much, but now and again a sigh does escape him. Then it came out, as a blow to Plumplington, that Polly too had a lover. And the last person in Plumplington who heard the news was Mr. Peppercorn. It seemed from his demeanour, when he first heard the tidings, that he had not expected that any such accident would ever happen. And yet Polly Peppercorn was a very pretty, bright girl of one-and-twenty of whom the wonder was,—if it was true,—that she had never already had a lover. She looked to be the very girl for lovers, and she looked also to be one quite able to keep a lover in his place.

Emily Greenmantle's lover was a two-months'-old story when Polly's lover became known to the public. There was a young man in Barchester who came over on Thursdays dealing with Mr. Peppercorn for malt. He was a fine stalwart young fellow, six-feet-one, with bright eyes and very light hair and whiskers, with a pair of shoulders which would think nothing of a sack of wheat, a hot temper, and a thoroughly good heart. It was known to all Plumplington that he had not a shilling in the world, and that he earned forty shillings a week from Messrs. Mealing's establishment at Barchester. Men said of him that he was likely to do well in the world, but nobody thought that he would have the impudence to make up to Polly Peppercorn.

But all the girls saw it and many of the old women, and some even of the men. And at last Polly told him that if he had anything to say to her he must say it to her father. 'And you mean to have him, then?' said Bessy Rolt in surprise. Her lover was by at the moment, though not exactly within hearing of Bessy's question. But Polly when she was alone with Bessy spoke up her mind freely. 'Of course I mean to have him, if he pleases. What else? You don't suppose I would go on with a young man like that and mean nothing. I hate such ways.'

'But what will your father say?'

'Why shouldn't he like it? I heard papa say that he had but 7s. 6d. a week when he first came to Du Boungs. He got poor mamma to marry him, and he never was a good-looking man.'

'But he had made some money.'

'Jack has made no money as yet, but he is a good-looking fellow. So they're quits. I believe that father would do anything for me, and when he knows that I mean it he won't let me break my heart.'

But a week after that a change had come over the scene. Jack had gone to Mr. Hickory Peppercorn, and Mr. Peppercorn had given him a rough word or two. Jack had not borne the rough word well, and old Hickory, as he was called, had said in his wrath, 'Impudent cub! you've got nothing. Do you know what my girl will have?'

'I've never asked.'

'You knew she was to have something.'

'I know nothing about it. I'm ready to take the rough and the smooth together. I'll marry the young lady and wait till you give her something.' Hickory couldn't turn him out on the spur of the moment because there was business to be done, but warned him not to go into his private house. 'If you speak another word to Polly, old as I am, I'll measure you across the back with my stick.' But Polly, who knew her father's temper, took care to keep out of her father's sight on that occasion.

Polly after that began the battle in a fashion that had been invented by herself. No one heard the words that were spoken between her and her father,—her father who had so idolized her; but it appeared to the people of Plumplington that Polly was holding her own. No disrespect was shown to her father, not a word was heard from her mouth that was not affectionate or at least decorous. But she took upon herself at once a certain lowering of her own social standing. She never drank tea with Emily Greenmantle, or accosted her in the street with her old friendly manner. She was terribly humble to Dr. Freeborn, who however would not acknowledge her humility on any account. 'What's come over you?' said the Doctor. 'Let me have none of your stage plays or I shall take you and shake you.'

'You can shake me if you like it, Dr. Freeborn,' said Polly, 'but I know who I am and what my position is.'

'You are a determined young puss,' said the Doctor, 'but I am not going to help you in opposing your own father.' Polly said not a word further, but looked very demure as the Doctor took his departure.

But Polly performed her greatest stroke in reference to a change in her dress. All her new silks, that had been the pride of her father's heart, were made to give way to old stuff gowns. People wondered where the old gowns, which had not been seen for years, had been stowed away. It was the same on Sundays as on Mondays and Tuesdays. But the due gradation was kept between Sundays and week-days. She was quite well enough dressed for a brewer's foreman's daughter on one day as on the other, but neither on one day nor on the other was she at all the Polly Peppercorn that Plumplington had known for the last couple of years. And there was not a word said about it. But all Plumplington knew that Polly was fitting herself, as regarded her outside garniture, to be the wife of Jack Hollycombe with 40s. a week. And all Plumplington said that she would carry her purpose, and that Hickory Peppercorn would break down under stress of the artillery brought to bear against him. He could not put out her clothes for her, or force her into wearing them as her mother might have done, had her mother been living. He could only tear his hair and greet, and swear to himself that under no such artillery as this would he give way. His girl should never marry Jack Hollycombe. He thought he knew his girl well enough to be sure that she would not marry without his consent. She might make him very unhappy by wearing dowdy clothes, but she would not quite break his heart. In the meantime Polly took care that her father should have no opportunity of measuring Jack's back.

With the affairs of Miss Greenmantle much more ceremony was observed, though I doubt whether there was more earnestness felt in the matter. Mr. Peppercorn was very much in earnest, as was Polly,—and Jack Hollycombe. But Peppercorn talked about it publicly, and Polly showed her purpose, and Jack exhibited the triumphant lover to all eyes. Mr. Greenmantle was silent as death in respect to the great trouble that had come upon him. He had spoken to no one on the subject except to the peccant lover, and just a word or two to old Dr. Freeborn. There was no trouble in the town that did not reach Dr. Freeborn's ears; and Mr. Greenmantle, in spite of his little jealousy, was no exception. To the Doctor he had said a word or two as to Emily's bad behaviour. But in the stiffness of his back, and the length of his face, and the continual frown which was gathered on his brows, he was eloquent to all the town. Peppercorn had no powers of looking as he looked. The gloom of the bank was awful. It was felt to be so by the two junior clerks, who hardly knew whether to hate or to pity most Mr. Philip Hughes. And if Mr. Greenmantle's demeanour was hard to bear down below, within the bank, what must it have been up-stairs in the family sitting-room? It was now, at this time, about the middle of November; and with Emily everything had been black and clouded for the last two months past. Polly's misfortune had only begun about the first of November. The two young ladies had had their own ideas about their own young men from nearly the same date. Philip Hughes and Jack Hollycombe had pushed themselves into prominence about the same time. But Emily's trouble had declared itself six weeks before Polly had sent her young man to her father. The first scene which took place with Emily and Mr. Greenmantle, after young Hughes had declared himself, was very impressive. 'What is this, Emily?'

'What is what, papa?' A poor girl when she is thus cross-questioned hardly knows what to say.

'One of the young men in the bank has been to me.' There was in this a great slur intended. It was acknowledged by all Plumplington that Mr. Hughes was the cashier, and was hardly more fairly designated as one of the young men than would have been Mr. Greenmantle himself,—unless in regard to age.

'Philip, I suppose,' said Emily. Now Mr. Greenmantle had certainly led the way into this difficulty himself. He had been allured by some modesty in the young man's demeanour,—or more probably by something pleasant in his manner which had struck Emily also,—to call him Philip. He had, as it were, shown a parental regard for him, and those who had best known Mr. Greenmantle had been sure that he would not forget his manifest good intentions towards the young man. As coming from Mr. Greenmantle the use of the christian name had been made. But certainly he had not intended that it should be taken up in this manner. There had been an ingratitude in it, which Mr. Greenmantle had felt very keenly.

'I would rather that you should call the young man Mr. Hughes in anything that you may have to say about him.'

'I thought you called him Philip, papa.'

'I shall never do so again,–never. What is this that he has said to me? Can it be true?'

'I suppose it is true, papa.'

'You mean that you want to marry him?'

'Yes, papa.'

'Goodness gracious me!' After this Emily remained silent for a while. 'Can you have realised the fact that the young man has–nothing; literally nothing!' What is a young lady to say when she is thus appealed to? She knew that though the young man had nothing, she would have a considerable portion of her own. She was her father's only child. She had not 'cared for' young Gresham, whereas she had 'cared for' young Hughes. What would be all the world to her if she must marry a man she did not care for? That, she was resolved, she would not do. But what would all the world be to her if she were not allowed to marry the man she did love? And what good would it be to her to be the only daughter of a rich man if she were to be baulked in this manner? She had thought it all over, assuming to herself perhaps greater privileges than she was entitled to expect.

But Emily Greenmantle was somewhat differently

circumstanced from Polly Peppercorn. Emily was afraid of her father's sternness, whereas Polly was not in the least afraid of her governor, as she was wont to call him. Old Hickory was, in a good-humoured way, afraid of Polly. Polly could order the things, in and about the house, very much after her own fashion. To tell the truth Polly had but slight fear but that she would have her own way, and when she laid by her best silks she did not do it as a person does bid farewell to those treasures which are not to be seen again. They could be made to do very well for the future Mrs. Hollycombe. At any rate, like a Marlborough or a Wellington, she went into the battle thinking of victory and not of defeat. But Wellington was a long time before he had beaten the French, and Polly thought that there might be some trouble also for her. With Emily there was no prospect of ultimate victory.

Mr. Greenmantle was a very stern man, who could look at his daughter as though he never meant to give way. And, without saying a word, he could make all Plumplington understand that such was to be the case. 'Poor Emily,' said the old Doctor to his old wife; 'I'm afraid there's a bad time coming for her.' 'He's a nasty cross old man,' said the old woman. 'It always does take three generations to make a "gentleman."' For Mrs. Freeborn's ancestors had come from the time of James I.

'You and I had better understand each other,' said Mr. Greenmantle, standing up with his back to the fireplace, and looking as though he were all poker from the top of his head to the heels of his boots. 'You cannot marry Mr. Philip Hughes.' Emily said nothing but turned her eyes down upon the ground. 'I don't suppose he thinks of doing so without money.'

'He has never thought about money at all.'

'Then what are you to live upon? Can you tell me that? He has £220 from the bank. Can you live upon that? Can you bring up a family?' Emily blushed as she still looked upon the ground. 'I tell you fairly that he shall never have the spending of my money. If you mean to desert me in my old age,–go.'

'Papa, you shouldn't say that.'

'You shouldn't think it.' Then Mr. Greenmantle looked as though he had uttered a clenching argument. 'You shouldn't think it. Now go away, Emily, and turn in your mind what I have said to you.'

CHAPTER TWO

'DOWN I SHALL GO'

THEN there came about a conversation between the two young ladies which was in itself very interesting. They had not met each other for about a fortnight when Emily Greenmantle came to Mr. Peppercorn's house. She had been thoroughly unhappy, and among her causes for sorrow had been the severance which seemed to have taken place between her and her friend. She had discussed all her troubles with Dr. Freeborn, and Dr. Freeborn had advised her to see Polly. 'Here's Christmas-time coming on and you are all going to quarrel among yourselves. I won't have any such nonsense. Go and see her.'

'It's not me, Dr. Freeborn,' said Emily. 'I don't want to quarrel with anybody; and there is nobody I like better than Polly.' Thereupon Emily went to Mr. Peppercorn's house when Peppercorn would be certainly at the brewery, and there she found Polly at home.

Polly was dressed very plainly. It was manifest to all eyes that the Polly Peppercorn of to-day was not the same Polly Peppercorn that had been seen about Plumplington for the last twelve months. It was equally manifest that Polly intended that everybody should see the difference. She had not meekly put on her poorer dress so that people should see that she was

[27]

no more than her father's child; but it was done with some ostentation. 'If father says that Jack and I are not to have his money I must begin to reduce myself by times.' That was what Polly intended to say to all Plumplington. She was sure that her father would have to give way under such shots as she could fire at him.

'Polly, I have not seen you, oh, for such a long time.'

Polly did not look like quarrelling at all. Nothing could be more pleasant than the tone of her voice. But yet there was something in her mode of address which at once excited Emily Greenmantle's attention. In bidding her visitor welcome she called her Miss Greenmantle. Now on that matter there had been some little trouble heretofore, in which the banker's daughter had succeeded in getting the better of the banker. He had suggested that Miss Peppercorn was safer than Polly; but Emily had replied that Polly was a nice dear girl, very much in Dr. Freeborn's good favours, and in point of fact that Dr. Freeborn wouldn't allow it. Mr. Greenmantle had frowned, but had felt himself unable to stand against Dr. Freeborn in such a matter. 'What's the meaning of the Miss Greenmantle?' said Emily sorrowfully.

'It's what I'm come to,' said Polly, without any show of sorrow, 'and it's what I mean to stick to as being my proper place. You have heard all about Jack Hollycombe. I suppose I ought to call him John as I'm speaking to you.'

'I don't see what difference it will make.'

'Not much in the long run; but yet it will make a

difference. It isn't that I should not like to be just the same to you as I have been, but father means to put me down in the world, and I don't mean to quarrel with him about that. Down I shall go.'

'And therefore I'm to be called Miss Greenmantle.'

'Exactly. Perhaps it ought to have been always so as I'm so poorly minded as to go back to such a one as Jack Hollycombe. Of course it is going back. Of course Jack is as good as father was at his age. But father has put himself up since that and has put me up. I'm such poor stuff that I wouldn't stay up. A girl has to begin where her husband begins; and as I mean to be Jack's wife I have to fit myself for the place.'

'I suppose it's the same with me, Polly.'

'Not quite. You're a lady bred and born, and Mr. Hughes is a gentleman. Father tells me that a man who goes about the country selling malt isn't a gentleman. I suppose father is right. But Jack is a good enough gentleman to my thinking. If he had a share of father's money he would break out in quite a new place.'

'Mr. Peppercorn won't give it to him?'

'Well! That's what I don't know. I do think the governor loves me. He is the best fellow anywhere for downright kindness. I mean to try him. And if he won't help me I shall go down as I say. You may be sure of this,—that I shall not give up Jack.'

'You wouldn't marry him against your father's wishes?'

Here Polly wasn't quite ready with her answer. 'I don't know that father has a right to destroy all my happiness,' she said at last. 'I shall wait a long time first at any rate. Then if I find that Jack can remain constant,—I don't know what I shall do.'

'What does he say?'

'Jack? He's all sugar and promises. They always are for a time. It takes a deal of learning to know whether a young man can be true. There is not above one in twenty that do come out true when they are tried.'

'I suppose not,' said Emily sorrowfully.

'I shall tell Mr. Jack that he's got to go through the ordeal. Of course he wants me to say that I'll marry him right off the reel and that he'll earn money enough for both of us. I told him only this morning —'

'Did you see him?'

'I wrote him,—out quite plainly. And I told him that there were other people had hearts in their bodies besides him and me. I'm not going to break father's heart,—not if I can help it. It would go very hard with him if I were to walk out of this house and marry Jack Hollycombe, quite plain like.'

'I would never do it,' said Emily with energy.

'You are a little different from me, Miss Greenmantle. I suppose my mother didn't think much about such things, and as long as she got herself married decent, didn't trouble herself much what her people said.'

[30]

'Didn't she?'

'I fancy not. Those sort of cares and bothers always come with money. Look at the two girls in this house. I take it they only act just like their mothers, and if they're good girls, which they are, they get their mothers' consent. But the marriage goes on as a matter of course. It's where money is wanted that parents become stern and their children become dutiful. I mean to be dutiful for a time. But I'd rather have Jack than father's money.'

'Dr. Freeborn says that you and I are not to quarrel. I am sure I don't see why we should.'

'What Dr. Freeborn says is very well.' It was thus that Polly carried on the conversation after thinking over the matter for a moment or two. 'Dr. Freeborn is a great man in Plumplington, and has his own way in everything. I'm not saying a word against Dr. Freeborn, and goodness knows I don't want to quarrel with you, Miss Greenmantle.'

'I hope not.'

'But I do mean to go down if father makes me, and if Jack proves himself a true man.'

'I suppose he'll do that,' said Miss Greenmantle. 'Of course you think he will.'

'Well, upon the whole I do,' said Polly. 'And though I think father will have to give up, he won't do it just at present, and I shall have to remain just as I am for a time.'

'And wear——' Miss Greenmantle had intended to inquire whether it was Polly's purpose to go about in her second-rate clothes, but had hesitated, not quite liking to ask the question.

'Just that,' said Polly. 'I mean to wear such clothes as shall be suitable for Jack's wife. And I mean to give up all my airs. I've been thinking a deal about it, and they're wrong. Your papa and my father are not the same.'

'They are not the same, of course,' said Emily.

'One is a gentleman, and the other isn't. That's the long and the short of it. I oughtn't to have gone to your house drinking tea and the rest of it; and I oughtn't to have called you Emily. That's the long and the short of that,' said she, repeating herself.

'Dr. Freeborn thinks—'

'Dr. Freeborn mustn't quite have it all his own way. Of course Dr. Freeborn is everything in Plumplington; and when I'm Jack's wife I'll do what he tells me again.'

'I suppose you'll do what Jack tells you then.'

'Well, yes; not exactly. If Jack were to tell me not to go to church,—which he won't,—I shouldn't do what he told me. If he said he'd like to have a leg of mutton boiled, I should boil it. Only legs of mutton wouldn't be very common with us, unless father comes round.'

'I don't see why all that should make a difference between you and me.'

'It will have to do so,' said Polly with perfect self-assurance. 'Father has told me that he doesn't mean to find money to buy legs of mutton for Jack Hollycombe. Those were his very words. I'm determined

I'll never ask him. And he said he wasn't going to find clothes for Jack Hollycombe's brats. I'll never go to him to find a pair of shoes for Jack Hollycombe or one of his brats. I've told Jack as much, and Jack says that I'm right. But there's no knowing what's inside a young man till you've tried him. Jack may fall off, and if so there's an end of him. I shall come round in time, and wear my fine clothes again when I settle down as an old maid. But father will never make me wear them, and I shall never call you anything but Miss Greenmantle, unless he consent to my marrying Jack.'

Such was the eloquence of Polly Peppercorn as spoken on that occasion. And she certainly did fill Miss Greenmantle's mind with a strong idea of her persistency. When Polly's last speech was finished the banker's daughter got up, and kissed her friend, and took her leave. 'You shouldn't do that,' said Polly with a smile. But on this one occasion she returned the caress; and then Miss Greenmantle went her way thinking over all that had been said to her.

'I'll do it too, let him persuade me ever so.' This was Polly's soliloquy to herself when she was left alone, and the 'him' spoken of on this occasion was her father. She had made up her own mind as to the line of action she would follow, and she was quite resolved never again to ask her father's permission for her marriage. Her father and Jack might fight that out among themselves, as best they could. There had already been one scene on the subject between herself

B

and her father in which the brewer's foreman had acted the part of stern parent with considerable violence. He had not beaten his girl, nor used bad words to her, nor, to tell the truth, had he threatened her with any deprivation of those luxuries to which she had become accustomed; but he had sworn by all the oaths which he knew by heart that if she chose to marry Jack Hollycombe she should go 'bare as a tinker's brat.' 'I don't want anything better,' Polly had said. 'He'll want something else though,' Peppercorn had replied, and had bounced out of the room and banged the door.

Miss Greenmantle, in whose nature there was perhaps something of the lugubrious tendencies which her father exhibited, walked away home from Mr. Peppercorn's house with a sad heart. She was very sorry for Polly Peppercorn's grief, and she was very sorry also for her own. But she had not that amount of high spirits which sustained Polly in her troubles. To tell the truth Polly had some hope that she might get the better of her father, and thereby do a good turn both to him and to herself. But Emily Greenmantle had but little hope. Her father had not sworn at her, nor had he banged the door, but he had pressed his lips together till there was no lip really visible. And he had raised his forehead on high till it looked as though one continuous poker descended from the crown of his head passing down through his entire body. 'Emily, it is out of the question. You had better leave me.' From that day to this not a word had been spoken on the 'subject.' Young Gresham had been once asked to dine at the bank, but that had been the only effort made by Mr. Greenmantle in the matter.

Emily had felt as she walked home that she had not at her command weapons so powerful as those which Polly intended to use against her father. No change in her dress would be suitable to her, and were she to make any it would be altogether inefficacious. Nor would her father be tempted by his passion to throw in her teeth the lack of either boots or legs of mutton which might be the consequence of her marriage with a poor man. There was something almost vulgar in these allusions which made Emily feel that there had been some reason for her papa's exclusiveness,—but she let that go by. Polly was a dear girl, though she had found herself able to speak of the brats' feet without even a blush. 'I suppose there will be brats, and why shouldn't she,—when she's talking only to me. It must be so I suppose.' So Emily had argued to herself, making the excuse altogether on behalf of her friend. But she was sure that if her father had heard Polly he would have been offended.

But what was Emily to do on her own behalf? Harry Gresham had come to dinner, but his coming had been altogether without effect. She was quite sure that she could never care for Harry Gresham, and she did not quite believe that Harry Gresham cared very much for her. There was a rumour about in the country that Harry Gresham wanted money, and she knew well that Harry Gresham's father and her own papa had

[35]

been closeted together. She did not care to be married after such a fashion as that. In truth Philip Hughes was the only young man for whom she did care.

She had always felt her father to be the most impregnable of men,–but now on this subject of her marriage he was more impregnable than ever. He had never yet entirely digested that poker which he had swallowed when he had gone so far as to tell his daughter that it was 'entirely out of the question.' From that hour her home had been terrible to her as a home, and had not been in the least enlivened by the presence of Harry Gresham. And now how was she to carry on the battle? Polly had her plans all drawn out, and was preparing herself for the combat seriously. But for Emily, there was no means left for fighting.

And she felt that though a battle with her father might be very proper for Polly, it would be highly unbecoming for herself. There was a difference in rank between herself and Polly of which Polly clearly understood the strength. Polly would put on her poor clothes, and go into the kitchen, and break her father's heart by preparing for a descent into regions which would be fitting for her were she to marry her young man without a fortune. But to Miss Greenmantle this would be impossible. Any marriage, made now or later, without her father's leave, seemed to her out of the question. She would only ruin her 'young man' were she to attempt it, and the attempt would be altogether inefficacious. She could only be unhappy, melancholy,– and perhaps morose; but she could not be so unhappy

[36]

and melancholy,—or morose, as was her father. At such weapons he could certainly beat her. Since that unhappy word had been spoken, the poker within him had not been for a moment lessened in vigour. And she feared even to appeal to Dr. Freeborn. Dr. Freeborn could do much,—almost everything in Plumplington,—but there was a point at which her father would turn even against Dr. Freeborn. She did not think that the Doctor would ever dare to take up the cudgels against her father on behalf of Philip Hughes. She felt that it would be more becoming for her to abstain and to suffer in silence than to apply to any human being for assistance. But she could be miserable;—outwardly miserable as well as inwardly;—and very miserable she was determined that she would be! Her father no doubt would be miserable too; but she was sad at heart as she bethought herself that her father would rather like it. Though he could not easily digest a poker when he had swallowed it, it never seemed to disagree with him. A state of misery in which he would speak to no one seemed to be almost to his taste. In this way poor Emily Greenmantle did not see her way to the enjoyment of a happy Christmas.

CHAPTER THREE

MR. GREENMANTLE IS MUCH PERPLEXED

THAT evening Mr. Greenmantle and his daughter sat down to dinner together in a very unhappy humour. They always dined at half-past seven; not that Mr. Greenmantle liked to have his dinner at that hour better than any other, but because it was considered to be fashionable. Old Mr. Gresham, Harry's father, always dined at half-past seven, and Mr. Greenmantle rather followed the habits of a county gentleman's life. He used to dine at this hour when there was a dinner-party, but of late he had adopted it for the family meal. To tell the truth there had been a few words between him and Dr. Freeborn while Emily had been talking over matters with Polly Peppercorn. Dr. Freeborn had not ventured to say a word as to Emily's love affairs; but had so discussed those of Jack Hollycombe and Polly as to leave a strong impression on the mind of Mr. Greenmantle. He had quite understood that the Doctor had been talking at himself, and that when Jack's name had been mentioned, or Polly's, the Doctor had intended that the wisdom spoken should be intended to apply to Emily and to Philip Hughes. 'It's only because he can give her a lot of money,' the Doctor had said. 'The young man is a good young man, and steady. What is Peppercorn that he should want anything better for his child? Young Hollycombe

[38]

has taken her fancy, and why shouldn't she have him?'

'I suppose Mr. Peppercorn may have his own views,' Mr. Greenmantle had answered.

'Bother his views,' the Doctor had said. 'He has no one else to think of but the girl and his views should be confined to making her happy. Of course he'll have to give way at last, and will only make himself ridiculous. I shouldn't say a word about it only that the young man is all that he ought to be.'

Now in this there was not a word which did not apply to Mr. Greenmantle himself. And the worst of it was the fact that Mr. Greenmantle felt that the Doctor intended it.

But as he had taken his constitutional walk before dinner, a walk which he took every day of his life after bank hours, he had sworn to himself that he would not be guided, or in the least affected, by Dr. Freeborn's opinion in the matter. There had been an underlying bitterness in the Doctor's words which had much aggravated the banker's ill-humour. The Doctor would not so have spoken of the marriage of one of his own daughters,—before they had all been married. Birth would have been considered by him almost before anything. The Peppercorns and the Greenmantles were looked down upon almost from an equal height. Now Mr. Greenmantle considered himself to be infinitely superior to Mr. Peppercorn, and to be almost, if not altogether, equal to Dr. Freeborn. He was much the richer man of the two, and his money was quite sufficient to outweigh a century or two of blood.

[39]

Peppercorn might do as he pleased. What became of Peppercorn's money was an affair of no matter. The Doctor's argument was no doubt good as far as Peppercorn was concerned. Peppercorn was not a gentleman. It was that which Mr. Greenmantle felt so acutely. The one great line of demarcation in the world was that which separated gentlemen from non-gentlemen. Mr. Greenmantle assured himself that he was a gentleman, acknowledged to be so by all the county. The old Duke of Omnium had customarily asked him to dine at his annual dinner at Gatherum Castle. He had been in the habit of staying occasionally at Greshambury, Mr. Gresham's county seat, and Mr. Gresham had been quite willing to forward the match between Emily and his younger son. There could be no doubt that he was on the right side of the line of demarcation. He was therefore quite determined that his daughter should not marry the Cashier in his own bank.

As he sat down to dinner he looked sternly at his daughter, and thought with wonder at the viciousness of her taste. She looked at him almost as sternly as she thought with awe of his cruelty. In her eyes Philip Hughes was quite as good a gentleman as her father. He was the son of a clergyman who was now dead, but had been intimate with Dr. Freeborn. And in the natural course of events might succeed her father as manager of the Bank. To be manager of the Bank at Plumplington was not very much in the eyes of the world; but it was the position which her father filled. Emily vowed to herself as she looked across the table

[40]

into her father's face, that she would be Mrs. Philip Hughes,—or remain unmarried all her life. 'Emily, shall I help you to a mutton cutlet?' said her father with solemnity.

'No thank you, papa,' she replied with equal gravity:

'On what then do you intend to dine?' There had been a sole of which she had also declined to partake. 'There is nothing else, unless you will dine off rice pudding.'

'I am not hungry, papa.' She could not decline to wear her customary clothes as did her friend Polly, but she could at any rate go without her dinner. Even a father so stern as was Mr. Greenmantle could not make her eat. Then there came a vision across her eyes of a long sickness, produced chiefly by inanition, in which she might wear her father's heart out. And then she felt that she might too probably lack the courage. She did not care much for her dinner; but she feared that she could not persevere to the breaking of her father's heart. She and her father were alone together in the world, and he in other respects had always been good to her. And now a tear trickled from her eye down her nose as she gazed upon the empty plate. He ate his two cutlets one after another in solemn silence and so the dinner was ended.

He, too, had felt uneasy qualms during the meal. 'What shall I do if she takes to starving herself and going to bed, all along of that young rascal in the outer bank?' It was thus that he had thought of it, and he too for a moment had begun to tell himself that

[41]

were she to be perverse she must win the battle. He knew himself to be strong in purpose, but he doubted whether he would be strong enough to stand by and see his daughter starve herself. A week's starvation or a fortnight's he might bear, and it was possible that she might give way before that time had come.

Then he retired to a little room inside the bank, a room that was half private and half official, to which he would betake himself to spend his evening whenever some especially gloomy fit would fall upon him. Here, within his own bosom, he turned over all the circumstances of the case. No doubt he had with him all the laws of God and man. He was not bound to give his money to any such interloper as was Philip Hughes. On that point he was quite clear. But what step had he better take to prevent the evil? Should he resign his position at the bank, and take his daughter away to live in the south of France? It would be a terrible step to which to be driven by his own Cashier. He was as efficacious to do the work of the bank as ever he had been, and he would leave this enemy to occupy his place. The enemy would then be in a condition to marry a wife without a fortune; and who could tell whether he might not show his power in such a crisis by marrying Emily! How terrible in such a case would be his defeat! At any rate he might go for three months on sick leave. He had been for nearly forty years in the bank, and had never yet been absent for a day on sick leave. Thinking of all this he remained alone till it was time for him to go to bed.

[42]

On the next morning he was dumb and stiff as ever, and after breakfast sat dumb and stiff, in his official room behind the bank counter, thinking over his great trouble. He had not spoken a word to Emily since yesterday's dinner beyond asking her whether she would take a bit of fried bacon. 'No thank you, papa,' she had said; and then Mr. Greenmantle had made up his mind that he must take her away somewhere at once, lest she should be starved to death. Then he went into the bank and sat there signing his name, and meditating the terrible catastrophe which was to fall upon him. Hughes, the Cashier, had become Mr. Hughes, and if any young man could be frightened out of his love by the stern look and sterner voice of a parent, Mr. Hughes would have been so frightened.

Then there came a knock at the door, and Mr. Peppercorn having been summoned to come in, entered the room. He had expressed a desire to see Mr. Green-mantle personally, and having proved his eagerness by a double request, had been allowed to have his way. It was quite a common affair for him to visit the bank on matters referring to the brewery; but now it was evident to any one with half an eye that such at present was not Mr. Peppercorn's business. He had on the clothes in which he habitually went to church instead of the light-coloured pepper and salt tweed jacket in which he was accustomed to go about among the malt and barrels. 'What can I do for you, Mr. Peppercorn?' said the banker. But the aspect was the aspect of a man who had a poker still fixed within his head and gullet.

''Tis nothing about the brewery, sir, or I shouldn't have troubled you. Mr. Hughes is very good at all that kind of thing.' A further frown came over Mr. Greenmantle's face, but he said nothing. 'You know my daughter Polly, Mr. Greenmantle?'

'I am aware that there is a Miss Peppercorn,' said the other. Peppercorn felt that an offence was intended. Mr. Greenmantle was of course aware. 'What can I do on behalf of Miss Peppercorn?'

'She's as good a girl as ever lived.'

'I do not in the least doubt it. If it be necessary that you should speak to me respecting Miss Peppercorn, will it not be well that you should take a chair?'

Then Mr. Peppercorn sat down, feeling that he had been snubbed. 'I may say that my only object in life is to do every mortal thing to make my girl happy.' Here Mr. Greenmantle simply bowed. 'We sit close to you in church, where, however, she comes much more reg'lar than me, and you must have observed her scores of times.'

'I am not in the habit of looking about among young ladies at church time, but I have occasionally been aware that Miss Peppercorn has been there.'

'Of course you have. You couldn't help it. Well, now, you know the sort of appearance she has made.'

'I can assure you, Mr. Peppercorn, that I have not observed Miss Peppercorn's dress in particular. I do not look much at the raiment worn by young ladies even in the outer world,–much less in church. I have a daughter of my own—'

'It's her as I'm coming to.' Then Mr. Greenmantle frowned more severely than ever. But the brewer did not at the moment say a word about the banker's daughter, but reverted to his own. 'You'll see next Sunday that my girl won't look at all like herself.'

'I really cannot promise—'

'You cannot help yourself, Mr. Greenmantle. I'll go bail that every one in church will see it. Polly is not to be passed over in a crowd;—at least she didn't used to be. Now it all comes of her wanting to get herself married to a young man who is altogether beneath her. Not as I mean to say anything against John Hollycombe as regards his walk of life. He is an industrious young man, as can earn forty shillings a week, and he comes over here from Barchester selling malt and such like. He may rise himself to £3 some of these days if he looks sharp about it. But I can give my girl—; well; what is quite unfit that he should think of looking for with a wife. And it's monstrous of Polly wanting to throw herself away in such a fashion. I don't believe in a young man being so covetous.'

'But what can I do, Mr. Peppercorn?'

'I'm coming to that. If you'll see her next Sunday you'll think of what my feelings must be. She's a-doing of it all just because she wants to show me that she thinks herself fit for nothing better than to be John Hollycombe's wife. When I tell her that I won't have it,—this sudden changing of her toggery, she says it's only fitting. It ain't fitting at all. I've got the money to buy things for her, and I'm willing to pay for it.

[45]

Is she to go poor just to break her father's heart?'

'But what can I do, Mr. Peppercorn?'

'I'm coming to that. The world does say, Mr. Greenmantle, that your young lady means to serve you in the same fashion.'

Hereupon Mr. Greenmantle waxed very wroth. It was terrible to his ideas that his daughter's affairs should be talked of at all by the people at Plumplington at large. It was worse again that his daughter and the brewer's girl should be lumped together in the scandal of the town. But it was worse, much worse, that this man Peppercorn should have dared to come to him, and tell him all about it. Did the man really expect that he, Mr. Greenmantle, should talk unreservedly as to the love affairs of his Emily? 'The world, Mr. Peppercorn, is very impertinent in its usual scandalous conversations as to its betters. You must forgive me if I do not intend on this occasion to follow the example of the world. Good morning, Mr. Peppercorn.'

'It's Dr. Freeborn as has coupled the two girls together.'

'I cannot believe it.'

'You ask him. It's he who has said that you and I are in a boat together.'

'I'm not in a boat with any man.'

'Well;—in a difficulty. It's the same thing. The Doctor seems to think that young ladies are to have their way in everything. I don't see it. When a man has made a tidy bit of money, as have you and I, he has a right to have a word to say as to who shall have the spending of it. A girl hasn't the right to say that she'll give it all to this man or to that. Of course, it's natural that my money should go to Polly. I'm not saying anything against it. But I don't mean that John Hollycombe shall have it. Now if you and I can put our heads together, I think we may be able to see our way out of the wood.'

'Mr. Peppercorn, I cannot consent to discuss with you the affairs of Miss Greenmantle.'

'But they're both alike. You must admit that.'

'I will admit nothing, Mr. Peppercorn.'

'I do think, you know, that we oughtn't to be done by our own daughters.'

'Really, Mr. Peppercorn—'

'Dr. Freeborn was saying that you and I would have to give way at last.'

'Dr. Freeborn knows nothing about it. If Dr. Freeborn coupled the two young ladies together he was I must say very impertinent; but I don't think he ever did so. Good morning, Mr. Peppercorn. I am fully engaged at present and cannot spare time for a longer interview.' Then he rose up from his chair, and leant upon the table with his hands by way of giving a certain signal that he was to be left alone. Mr. Peppercorn, after pausing a moment, searching for an opportunity for another word, was overcome at last by the rigid erectness of Mr. Greenmantle and withdrew.

CHAPTER FOUR

JACK HOLLYCOMBE

MR. Peppercorn's visit to the bank had been no doubt inspired by Dr. Freeborn. The Doctor had not actually sent him to the bank, but had filled his mind with the idea that such a visit might be made with good effect. 'There are you two fathers going to make two fools of yourselves,' the Doctor had said. 'You have each of you got a daughter as good as gold, and are determined to break their hearts because you won't give your money to a young man who happens to want it.'

'Now, Doctor, do you mean to tell me that you would have married your young ladies to the first young man that came and asked for them?'

'I never had much money to give my girls, and the men who came happened to have means of their own.'

'But if you'd had it, and if they hadn't, do you mean to tell me you'd never have asked a question?'

'A man should never boast that in any circumstances of his life he would have done just what he ought to do,—much less when he has never been tried. But if the lover be what he ought to be in morals and all that kind of thing, the girl's father ought not to refuse to help them. You may be sure of this,—that Polly means to have her own way. Providence has blessed you with a girl that knows her own mind.' On receipt of this compliment Mr. Peppercorn scratched his head. 'I wish I could say as much for my friend Greenmantle. You two are in a boat together, and ought to make up your mind as to what you should do.' Peppercorn resolved that he would remember the phrase about the boat, and began to think that it might be good that he should see Mr. Greenmantle. 'What on earth is it you two want? It is not as though you were dukes, and looking for proper alliances for two ducal spinsters.'

Now there had no doubt been a certain amount of intended venom in this. Dr. Freeborn knew well the weak points in Mr. Greenmantle's character, and was determined to hit him where he was weakest. He did not see the difference between the banker and the brewer nearly so clearly as did Mr. Greenmantle. He would probably have said that the line of demarcation came just below himself. At any rate, he thought that he would be doing best for Emily's interest if he made her father feel that all the world was on her side. Therefore it was that he so contrived that Mr. Peppercorn should pay his visit to the bank.

On his return to the brewery the first person that Peppercorn saw standing in the doorway of his own little sanctum was Jack Hollycombe. 'What is it you're wanting?' he asked gruffly.

'I was just desirous of saying a few words to yourself, Mr. Peppercorn.'

'Well, here I am!' There were two or three brewers and porters about the place, and Jack did not feel that he could plead his cause well in their presence. 'What is it you've got to say,—because I'm busy? There ain't no malt wanted for the next week; but you know that, and as we stand at present you can send it in without any more words, as it's needed.'

'It ain't about malt or anything of that kind.'

'Then I don't know what you've got to say. I'm very busy just at present, as I told you.'

'You can spare me five minutes inside.'

'No I can't.' But then Peppercorn resolved that neither would it suit him to carry on the conversation respecting his daughter in the presence of the work-men, and he thought that he perceived that Jack Holly-combe would be prepared to do so if he were driven. 'Come in if you will,' he said; 'we might as well have it out.' Then he led the way into the room, and shut the door as soon as Jack had followed him. 'Now what is it you have got to say? I suppose it's about that young woman down at my house.'

'It is, Mr. Peppercorn.'

'Then let me tell you that the least said will be soonest mended. She's not for you,—with my consent. And to tell you the truth I think that you have a mortal deal of brass coming to ask for her. You've no edication suited to her edication,—and what's wus, no money.' Jack had shown symptoms of anger when his deficient education had been thrown in his teeth, but had cheered up somewhat when the lack of money had been insisted upon. 'Them two things are so against you that you haven't a leg to stand on. My word! what do you expect that I should say when such a one as you comes a-courting to a girl like that?'

'I did, perhaps, think more of what she might say.'

'I daresay; – because you knew her to be a fool like yourself. I suppose you think yourself to be a very handsome young man.'

'I think she's a very handsome young woman. As to myself I never asked the question.'

'That's all very well. A man can always say as much as that for himself. The fact is you're not going to have her.'

'That's just what I want to speak to you about, Mr. Peppercorn.'

'You're not going to have her. Now I've spoken my intentions, and you may as well take one word as a thousand. I'm not a man as was ever known to change my mind when I'd made it up in such a matter as this.'

'She's got a mind too, Mr. Peppercorn.'

'She have, no doubt. She have a mind and so have you. But you haven't either of you got the money. The money is here,' and Mr. Peppercorn slapped his breeches pocket. 'I've had to do with earning it, and I mean to have to do with giving it away. To me there is no idea of honesty at all in a chap like you coming and asking a girl to marry you just because you know that she's to have a fortune.'

'That's not my reason.'

'It's uncommon like it. Now you see there's somebody else that's got to be asked. You think I'm a good-natured fellow. So I am, but I'm not soft like that.

'I never thought anything of the kind, Mr. Peppercorn.'

'Polly told you so, I don't doubt. She's right in thinking so, because I'd give Polly anything in reason. Or out of reason for the matter of that, because she is the apple of my eye.' This was indiscreet on the part of Mr. Peppercorn, as it taught the young man to think that he himself must be in reason or out of reason, and that in either case Polly ought to be allowed to have him. 'But there's one thing I stop at; and that is a young man who hasn't got either edication, or money,—nor yet manners.'

'There's nothing against my manner, I hope, Mr. Peppercorn.'

'Yes; there is. You come a-interfering with me in the most delicate affair in the world. You come into my family, and want to take away my girl. That I take it is the worst of manners.'

'How is any young lady to get married unless some young fellow comes after her?'

'There'll be plenty to come after Polly. You leave Polly alone, and you'll find that she'll get a young man suited to her. It's like your impudence to suppose that there's no other young man in the world so good as you. Why;—dash my wig; who are you? What are you? You're merely acting for them corn-factors over at Barsester.'

'And you're acting for them brewers here at Plumplington. What's the difference?'

'But I've got the money in my pocket, and you've got none. That's the difference. Put that in your pipe and smoke it. Now if you'll please to remember that

[52]

I'm very busy, you'll walk yourself off. You've had it out with me, which I didn't intend; and I've explained my mind very fully. She's not for you;—at any rate my money's not.'

'Look here, Mr. Peppercorn.'

'Well?'

'I don't care a farthing for your money.'

'Don't you, now?'

'Not in the way of comparing it with Polly herself. Of course money is a very comfortable thing. If Polly's to be my wife—'

'Which she ain't.'

'I should like her to have everything that a lady can desire.'

'How kind you are.'

'But in regard to money for myself I don't value it that.' Here Jack Hollycombe snapped his fingers. 'My meaning is to get the girl I love.'

'Then you won't.'

'And if she's satisfied to come to me without a shilling, I'm satisfied to take her in the same fashion. I don't know how much you've got, Mr. Peppercorn, but you can go and found a Hiram's Hospital with every penny of it.' At this moment a discussion was going on respecting a certain charitable institution in Barchester,—and had been going on for the last forty years,—as to which Mr. Hollycombe was here expressing the popular opinion of the day. 'That's the kind of thing a man should do who don't choose to leave his money to his own child.' Jack was now angry,

having had his deficient education twice thrown in his
teeth by one whom he conceived to be so much less
educated than himself. 'What I've got to say to you,
Mr. Peppercorn, is that Polly means to have me, and
if she's got to wait–why, I'm so minded that I'll wait
for her as long as ever she'll wait for me.' So saying
Jack Hollycombe left the room.

Mr. Peppercorn thrust his hat back upon his head,
and stood with his back to the fire, with the tails of his
coat appearing over his hands in his breeches pockets,
glaring out of his eyes with anger which he did not care
to suppress. This man had presented to him a picture
of his future life which was most unalluring. There was
nothing he desired less than to give his money to such
an abominable institution as Hiram's Hospital. Polly,
his own dear daughter Polly, was intended to be the
recipient of all his savings. As he went about among
the beer barrels, he had been a happy man as he
thought of Polly bright with the sheen which his
money had provided for her. But it was of Polly
married to some gentleman that he thought at these
moments;–of Polly surrounded by a large family of little
gentlemen and little ladies. They would all call him
grandpapa; and in the evenings of his days he would
sit by the fire in that gentleman's parlour, a welcome
guest because of the means which he had provided;
and the little gentlemen and the little ladies would
surround him with their prattle and their noises and
caresses. He was not a man whom his intimates would
have supposed to be gifted with a strong imagination,

but there was the picture firmly set before his mind's eye. 'Edication,' however, in the intended son-in-law was essential. And the son-in-law must be a gentleman. Now Jack Hollycombe was not a gentleman, and was not educated up to that pitch which was necessary for Polly's husband.

But Mr. Peppercorn, as he thought of it all, was well aware that Polly had a decided will of her own. And he knew of himself that his own will was less strong than his daughter's. In spite of all the severe things which he had just said to Jack Hollycombe, there was present to him a dreadful weight upon his heart, as he thought that Polly would certainly get the better of him. At this moment he hated Jack Hollycombe with most un-Christian rancour. No misfortune that could happen to Jack, either sudden death, or forgery with flight to the antipodes, or loss of his good looks,– which Mr. Peppercorn most unjustly thought would be equally efficacious with Polly,–would at the present moment of his wrath be received otherwise than as a special mark of good-fortune. And yet he was well aware that if Polly were to come and tell him that she had by some secret means turned herself into Mrs. Jack Hollycombe, he knew very well that for Polly's sake he would have to take Jack with all his faults, and turn him into the dearest son-in-law that the world could have provided for him. This was a very trying position, and justified him in standing there for a quarter of an hour with his back to the fire, and his coat-tails over his arms, as they were thrust into his trousers pockets.

In the meantime Jack had succeeded in obtaining a few minutes' talk with Polly,—or rather the success had been on Polly's side, for she had managed the business. On coming out from the brewery Jack had met her in the street, and had been taken home by her. 'You might as well come in, Jack,' she had said, 'and have a few words with me. You have been talking to father about it, I suppose.'

'Well; I have. He says I am not sufficiently educated. I suppose he wants to get some young man from the colleges.'

'Don't you be stupid, Jack. You want to have your own way, I suppose.'

'I don't want him to tell me I'm uneducated. Other men that I've heard of ain't any better off than I am.'

'You mean himself,—which isn't respectful.'

'I'm educated up to doing what I've got to do. If you don't want more, I don't see what he's got to do with it.'

'As the times go of course a man should learn more and more. You are not to compare him to yourself; and it isn't respectful. If you want to say sharp things against him, Jack, you had better give it all up;—for I won't bear it.'

'I don't want to say anything sharp.'

'Why can't you put up with him? He's not going to have his own way. And he is older than you. And it is he that has got the money. If you care about it—'

'You know I care.'

'Very well. Suppose I do know, and suppose I don't.

I hear you say you do, and that's all I've got to act upon. Do you bide your time if you've got the patience, and all will come right. I shan't at all think so much of you if you can't bear a few sharp words from him.

'He may say whatever he pleases.'

'You ain't educated,—not like Dr. Freeborn, and men of that class.'

'What do I want with it?' said he.

'I don't know that you do want it. At any rate I don't want it; and that's what you've got to think about at present. You just go on, and let things be as they are. You don't want to be married in a week's time.'

'Why not?' he asked.

'At any rate I don't; and I don't mean to. This time five years will do very well.'

'Five years! You'll be an old woman.'

'The fitter for you, who'll still be three years older. If you've patience to wait leave it to me.'

'I haven't over much patience.'

'Then go your own way and suit yourself elsewhere.'

'Polly, you're enough to break a man's heart. You know that I can't go and suit myself elsewhere. You are all the world to me, Polly.'

'Not half so much as a quarter of malt if you could get your own price for it. A young woman is all very well just as a play-thing; but business is business;— isn't it, Jack?'

'Five years! Fancy telling a fellow that he must wait five years.'

'That'll do for the present, Jack. I'm not going to keep you here idle all the day. Father will be angry when I tell him that you've been here at all.'

'It was you that brought me.'

'Yes, I did. But you're not to take advantage of that. Now I say, Jack, hands off. I tell you I won't. I'm not going to be kissed once a week for five years. Well. Mark my words, this is the last time I ever ask you in here. No; I won't have it. Go away.' Then she succeeded in turning him out of the room and closing the house door behind his back. 'I think he's the best young man I see about anywhere. Father twits him about his education. It's my belief there's nothing he can't do that he's wanted for. That's the kind of education a man ought to have. Father says it's because he's handsome I like him. It does go a long way, and he is handsome. Father has got ideas of fashion into his head which will send him crazy before he has done with them.' Such was the soliloquy in which Miss Peppercorn indulged as soon as she had been left by her lover.

'Educated! Of course I'm not educated. I can't talk Latin and Greek as some of those fellows pretend to,– though for the matter of that I never heard it. But two and two make four, and ten and ten make twenty. And if a fellow says that it don't he is trying on some dishonest game. If a fellow understands that, and sticks to it, he has education enough for my business,– or for Peppercorn's either.' Then he walked back to the inn yard where he had left his horse and trap.

As he drove back to Barchester he made up his mind

that Polly Peppercorn would be worth waiting for. There was the memory of that kiss upon his lips which had not been made less sweet by the severity of the words which had accompanied it. The words indeed had been severe; but there had been an intention and a purpose about the kiss which had altogether redeemed the words. 'She is just one in a thousand, that's about the truth. And as for waiting for her;— I'll wait like grim death, only I hope it won't be necessary!' It was thus he spoke of the lady of his love as he drove himself into the town under Barchester Towers.

CHAPTER FIVE

DR. FREEBORN AND PHILIP HUGHES

THINGS went on at Plumplington without any
change for a fortnight,—that is without any change
for the better. But in truth the ill-humour both of Mr.
Greenmantle and of Mr. Peppercorn had increased to
such a pitch as to add an additional blackness to the
general haziness and drizzle and gloom of the November weather. It was now the end of November, and
Dr. Freeborn was becoming a little uneasy because
the Christmas attributes for which he was desirous
were still altogether out of sight. He was a man
specially anxious for the mundane happiness of his
parishioners and who would take any amount of per-
sonal trouble to insure it; but he was in fault perhaps
in this, that he considered that everybody ought to be
happy just because he told them to be so. He belonged
to the Church of England certainly, but he had no
dislike to Papists or Presbyterians, or dissenters in
general, as long as they would arrange themselves
under his banner as 'Freebornites.' And he had such
force of character that in Plumplington,—beyond which
he was not ambitious that his influence should extend,—
he did in general prevail. But at the present moment
he was aware that Mr. Greenmantle was in open
mutiny. That Peppercorn would yield he had strong
hope. Peppercorn he knew to be a weak, good fellow,
whose affection for his daughter would keep him right

at last. But until he could extract that poker from Mr.
Greenmantle's throat, he knew that nothing could be
done with him.

At the end of the fortnight Mr. Greenmantle called
at the Rectory about half an hour before dinner time,
when he knew that the Doctor would be found in his
study before going up to dress for dinner. 'I hope I am
not intruding, Dr. Freeborn,' he said. But the rust of
the poker was audible in every syllable as it fell from
his mouth.

'Not in the least. I've a quarter of an hour before I
go and wash my hands.'

'It will be ample. In a quarter of an hour I shall be
able sufficiently to explain my plans.' Then there was
a pause, as though Mr. Greenmantle had expected that
the explanation was to begin with the Doctor. 'I am
thinking,' the banker continued after a while, 'of taking
my family abroad to some foreign residence.' Now it
was well known to Dr. Freeborn that Mr. Greenmantle's family consisted exclusively of Emily.

'Going to take Emily away?' he said.

'Such is my purpose,—and myself also.'

'What are they to do at the bank?'

'That will be the worst of it, Dr. Freeborn. The bank
will be the great difficulty.'

'But you don't mean that you are going for good?'

'Only for a prolonged foreign residence;—that is to
say for six months. For forty years I have given but
very little trouble to the Directors. For forty years I
have been at my post and have never suggested any

prolonged absence. If the Directors cannot bear with me after forty years I shall think them unreasonable men.' Now in truth Mr. Greenmantle knew that the Directors would make no opposition to anything that he might propose; but he always thought it well to be armed with some premonitory grievance. 'In fact my pecuniary matters are so arranged that should the Directors refuse I shall go all the same.'

'You mean that you don't care a straw for the Directors.'

'I do not mean to postpone my comfort to their views,—or my daughter's.'

'But why does your daughter's comfort depend on your going away? I should have thought that she would have preferred Plumplington at present.'

That was true, no doubt. And Mr. Greenmantle felt;—well; that he was not exactly telling the truth in putting the burden of his departure upon Emily's comfort. If Emily, at the present crisis of affairs, were carried away from Plumplington for six months, her comfort would certainly not be increased. She had already been told that she was to go, and she had clearly understood why. 'I mean as to her future welfare,' said Mr. Greenmantle very solemnly.

Dr. Freeborn did not care to hear about the future welfare of young people. What had to be said as to their eternal welfare he thought himself quite able to say. After all there was something of benevolent paganism in his disposition. He liked better to deal with their present happiness,—so that there was nothing immoral in it. As to the world to come he thought that the fathers and mothers of his younger flock might safely leave that consideration to him. 'Emily is a remarkably good girl. That's my idea of her.'

Mr. Greenmantle was offended even at this. Dr. Freeborn had no right, just at present, to tell him that his daughter was a good girl. Her goodness had been greatly lessened by the fact that in regard to her marriage she was anxious to run counter to her father. 'She is a good girl. At least I hope so.'

'Do you doubt it?'

'Well, no;—or rather yes. Perhaps I ought to say no as to her life in general.'

'I should think so. I don't know what a father may want,—but I should think so. I never knew her miss church yet,—either morning or evening.'

'As far as that goes she does not neglect her duties.'

'What is the matter with her that she is to be taken off to some foreign climate for prolonged residence?' The Doctor among his other idiosyncrasies entertained an idea that England was the proper place for all Englishmen and Englishwomen who were not driven out of it by stress of pecuniary circumstances. 'Has she got a bad throat or a weak chest?'

'It is not on the score of her own health that I propose to move her,' said Mr. Greenmantle.

'You did say her comfort. Of course that may mean that she likes the French way of living. I did hear that we were to lose your services for a time, because you could not trust your own health.'

[63]

'It is failing me a little, Dr. Freeborn. I am already very near sixty.'

'Ten years my junior,' said the Doctor.

'We cannot all hope to have such perfect health as you possess.'

'I have never frittered it away,' said the Doctor, 'by prolonged residence in foreign parts.' This quotation of his own words was most harassing to Mr. Greenmantle, and made him more than once inclined to bounce in anger out of the Doctor's study. 'I suppose the truth is that Miss Emily is disposed to run counter to your wishes in regard to her marriage, and that she is to be taken away not from consumption or a weak throat, but from a dangerous lover.' Here Mr. Greenmantle's face became black as thunder. 'You see, Greenmantle, there is no good in our talking about this matter unless we understand each other.'

'I do not intend to give my girl to the young man upon whom she thinks that her affections rest.'

'I suppose she knows.'

'No, Dr. Freeborn. It is often the case that a young lady does not know; she only fancies, and where that is the case absence is the best remedy. You have said that Emily is a good girl.'

'A very good girl.'

'I am delighted to hear you so express yourself. But obedience to parents is a trait in character which is generally much thought of. I have put by a little money, Dr. Freeborn.'

'All Plumplington knows that.'

[64]

'And I shall choose that it shall go somewhat in accordance with my wishes. The young man of whom she is thinking—'

'Philip Hughes, an excellent fellow. I've known him all my life. He doesn't come to church quite so regularly as he ought, but that will be mended when he's married.'

'Hasn't got a shilling in the world,' continued Mr. Greenmantle, finishing his sentence. 'Nor is he—just,—just—just what I should choose for the husband of my daughter. I think that when I have said so he should take my word for it.'

'That's not the way of the world, you know.'

'It's the way of my world, Dr. Freeborn. It isn't often that I speak out, but when I do it's about something that I've a right to speak of. I've heard this affair of my daughter talked about all over the town. There was one Mr. Peppercorn came to me—'

'One Mr. Peppercorn? Why, Hickory Peppercorn is as well known in Plumplington as the church-steeple.'

'I beg your pardon, Dr. Freeborn; but I don't find any reason in that for his interfering about my daughter. I must say that I took it as a great piece of impertinence. Goodness gracious me! If a man's own daughter isn't to be considered peculiar to himself I don't know what is. If he'd asked you about your daughters,—before they were married?' Dr. Freeborn did not answer this, but declared to himself that neither Mr. Peppercorn nor Mr. Greenmantle could have taken such a liberty. Mr. Greenmantle evidently was not aware of it, but in truth

C

Dr. Freeborn and his family belonged altogether to another set. So at least Dr. Freeborn told himself. 'I've come to you now, Dr. Freeborn, because I have not liked to leave Plumplington for a prolonged residence in foreign parts without acquainting you.'

'I should have thought that unkind.'

'You are very good. And as my daughter will of course go with me, and as this idea of a marriage on her part must be entirely given up; –' the emphasis was here placed with much weight on the word entirely; –'I should take it as a great kindness if you would let my feelings on the subject be generally known. I will own that I should not have cared to have my daughter talked about, only that the mischief has been done.'

'In a little place like this,' said the Doctor, 'a young lady's marriage will always be talked about.'

'But the young lady in this case isn't going to be married.'

'What does she say about it herself?'

'I haven't asked her, Dr. Freeborn. I don't mean to ask her. I shan't ask her.'

'If I understand her feelings, Greenmantle, she is very much set upon it.'

'I cannot help it.'

'You mean to say then that you intend to condemn her to unhappiness merely because this young man hasn't got as much money at the beginning of his life as you have at the end of yours?'

'He hasn't got a shilling,' said Mr. Greenmantle.

'Then why can't you give him a shilling? What do you mean to do with your money?' Here Mr. Green-mantle again looked offended. 'You come and ask me, and I am bound to give you my opinion for what it's worth. What do you mean to do with your money? You're not the man to found a Hiram's Hospital with it. As sure as you are sitting there your girl will have it when you're dead. Don't you know that she will have it?'

'I hope so.'

'And because she's to have it, she's to be made wretched about it all her life. She's to remain an old maid, or else to be married to some well-born pauper, in order that you may talk about your son-in-law. Don't get into a passion, Greenmantle, but only think whether I'm not telling you the truth. Hughes isn't a spendthrift.'

'I have made no accusation against him.'

'Nor a gambler, nor a drunkard, nor is he the sort of man to treat a wife badly. He's there at the bank so that you may keep him under your own eye. What more on earth can a man want in a son-in-law?'

Blood, thought Mr. Greenmantle to himself; an old family name; county associations, and a certain some-thing which he felt quite sure Philip Hughes did not possess. And he knew well enough that Dr. Freeborn had married his own daughters to husbands who possessed these gifts; but he could not throw the fact back into the Rector's teeth. He was in some way conscious that the Rector had been entitled to expect so much for his girls, and that he, the banker, was not so entitled. The same idea passed through the Rector's mind. But the Rector knew how far the banker's courage would carry him. 'Good night, Dr. Freeborn,' said Mr. Greenmantle suddenly.

'Good night, Greenmantle. Shan't I see you again before you go?' To this the banker made no direct answer, but at once took his leave.

'That man is the greatest ass in all Plumplington,' the Doctor said to his wife within five minutes of the time of which the hall door was closed behind the banker's back. 'He's got an idea into his head about having some young county swell for his son-in-law.'

'Harry Gresham. Harry is too idle to earn money by a profession and therefore wants Greenmantle's money to live upon. There's Peppercorn wants something of the same kind for Polly. People are such fools.' But Mrs. Freeborn's two daughters had been married much after the same fashion. They had taken husbands nearly as old as their father, because Dr. Freeborn and his wife had thought much of 'blood.'

On the next morning Philip Hughes was summoned by the banker into the more official of the two back parlours. Since he had presumed to signify his love for Emily, he had never been asked to enjoy the familiarity of the other chamber. 'Mr. Hughes, you may probably have heard it asserted that I am about to leave Plumplington for a prolonged residence in foreign parts.' Mr. Hughes had heard it and so declared. 'Yes, Mr. Hughes, I am about to proceed to the south of France. My daughter's health requires attention,—and indeed on my own behalf I am in need of some change as well. I have not as yet officially made known my views to the Directors.'

'There will be, I should think, no impediment with them.'

'I cannot say. But at any rate I shall go. After forty years of service in the Bank I cannot think of allowing the peculiar views of men who are all younger than myself to interfere with my comfort. I shall go.'

'I suppose so, Mr. Greenmantle.'

'I shall go. I say it without the slightest disrespect for the Board. But I shall go.'

'Will it be permanent, Mr. Greenmantle?'

'That is a question which I am not prepared to answer at a moment's notice. I do not propose to move my furniture for six months. It would not, I believe, be within the legal power of the Directors to take possession of the Bank house for that period.'

'I am quite sure they would not wish it.'

'Perhaps my assurance on that subject may be of more avail. At any rate they will not remove me. I should not have troubled you on this subject were it not that your position in the Bank must be affected more or less.'

'I suppose that I could do the work for six months,' said Philip Hughes.

But this was a view of the case which did not at all suit Mr. Greenmantle's mind. His own duties at Plumplington had been, to his thinking, the most important ever confided to a Bank Manager. There was a peculiarity about Plumplington of which no one knew the intricate details but himself. The man did not exist who could do the work as he had done it. But still he had determined to go, and the work must be intrusted to some man of lesser competence. 'I should think it probable,' he said, 'that some confidential clerk will be sent over from Barchester. Your youth, Mr. Hughes, is against you. It is not for me to say what line the Directors may determine to take.'

'I know the people better than any one can do in Barchester.'

'Just so. But you will excuse me if I say you may for that reason be the less efficient. I have thought it expedient, however, to tell you of my views. If you have any steps that you wish to take you can now take them.'

Then Mr. Greenmantle paused, and had apparently brought the meeting to an end. But there was still something which he wished to say. He did think that by a word spoken in due season,—by a strong determined word, he might succeed in putting an end to this young man's vain and ambitious hopes. He did not wish to talk to the young man about his daughter; but, if the strong word might avail here was the opportunity. 'Mr. Hughes,' he began.

'Yes, sir.'

'There is a subject on which perhaps it would be well that I should be silent.' Philip, who knew the manager thoroughly, was now aware of what was coming, and thought it wise that he should say nothing at the moment. 'I do not know that any good can be done by speaking of it.' Philip still held his tongue. 'It is a matter no doubt of extreme delicacy,—of the most extreme delicacy I may say. If I go abroad as I intend, I shall as a matter of course take with me— Miss Greenmantle.'

'I suppose so.'

'I shall take with me—Miss Greenmantle. It is not to be supposed that when I go abroad for a prolonged sojourn in foreign parts, that I should leave—Miss Greenmantle behind me.'

'No doubt she will accompany you.'

'Miss Greenmantle will accompany me. And it is not improbable that my prolonged residence may in her case be—still further prolonged. It may be possible that she should link her lot in life to some gentleman whom she may meet in those realms.'

'I hope not,' said Philip.

'I do not think that you are justified, Mr. Hughes, in hoping anything in reference to my daughter's fate in life.'

'All the same, I do.'

'It is very,—very,—! I do not wish to use strong language, and therefore I will not say impertinent.'

'What am I to do when you tell me that she is to marry a foreigner?'

'I never said so. I never thought so. A foreigner! Good heavens! I spoke of a gentleman whom she might chance to meet in those realms. Of course I meant an English gentleman.'

[71]

'The truth is, Mr. Greenmantle, I don't want your daughter to marry anyone unless she can marry me.'

'A most selfish proposition.'

'It's a sort of matter in which a man is apt to be selfish, and it's my belief that if she were asked she'd say the same thing. Of course you can take her abroad and you can keep her there as long as you please.'

'I can;—and I mean to do it.'

'I am utterly powerless to prevent you, and so is she. In this contention between us I have only one point in my favour.'

'You have no point in your favour, sir.'

'The young lady's good wishes. If she be not on my side,—why then I am nowhere. In that case you needn't trouble yourself to take her out of Plumplington. But if—'

'You may withdraw, Mr. Hughes,' said the banker. 'The interview is over.' Then Philip Hughes withdrew, but as he went he shut the door after him in a very confident manner.

CHAPTER SIX

THE YOUNG LADIES ARE TO BE
TAKEN ABROAD

HOW should Philip Hughes see Emily before she had been carried away to 'foreign parts' by her stern father? As he regarded the matter it was absolutely imperative that he should do so. If she should be made to go, in her father's present state of mind, without having reiterated her vows, she might be persuaded by that foreign-living English gentleman whom she would find abroad, to give him her hand. Emily had no doubt confessed her love to Philip, but she had not done so in that bold unshrinking manner which had been natural to Polly Peppercorn. And her lover felt it to be incumbent upon him to receive some renewal of her assurance before she was taken away for a prolonged residence abroad. But there was a difficulty as to this. If he were to knock at the door of the private house and ask for Miss Greenmantle, the servant, though she was in truth Philip's friend in the matter, would not dare to show him up. The whole household was afraid of Mr. Greenmantle, and would receive any hint that his will was to be set aside with absolute dismay. So Philip at last determined to take the bull by the horns and force his way into the drawing-room. Mr. Greenmantle could not be made more hostile than he was; and then it was quite on the cards, that he might be kept in ignorance of the intrusion. When therefore the banker was sitting in his own more private room, Philip passed through from the bank into the house, and made his way up-stairs with no one to announce him.

With no one to announce him he passed straight through into the drawing-room, and found Emily sitting very melancholy over a half-knitted stocking. It had been commenced with an idea that it might perhaps be given to Philip, but as her father's stern severity had been announced she had given up that fond idea, and had increased the size, so as to fit them for the paternal feet. 'Good gracious, Philip,' she exclaimed, 'how on earth did you get here?'

'I came up-stairs from the bank.'

'Oh, yes; of course. But did you not tell Mary that you were coming?'

'I should never have been let up had I done so. Mary has orders not to let me put my foot within the house.'

'You ought not to have come; indeed you ought not.'

'And I was to let you go abroad without seeing you! Was that what I ought to have done? It might be that I should never see you again. Only think of what my condition must be.'

'Is not mine twice worse?'

'I do not know. If it be twice worse than mine then I am the happiest man in all the world.'

'Oh, Philip, what do you mean?'

'If you will assure me of your love—'

'I have assured you.'

'Give me another assurance, Emily,' he said, sitting down beside her on the sofa. But she started up quickly to her feet. 'When you gave me the assurance before, then – then—'

'One assurance such as that ought to be quite enough.'

'But you are going abroad.'

'That can make no difference.'

'Your father says, that you will meet there some Englishman who will—'

'My father knows nothing about it. I shall meet no Englishman, and no foreigner; at least none that I shall care about. You oughtn't to get such an idea into your head.'

'That's all very well, but how am I to keep such ideas out? Of course there will be men over there; and if you come across some idle young fellow who has not his bread to earn as I do, won't it be natural that you should listen to him?'

'No, it won't be natural.'

'It seems to me to be so. What have I got that you should continue to care for me?'

'You have my word, Philip. Is that nothing?' She had now seated herself on a chair away from the sofa, and he, feeling at the time some special anxiety to get her into his arms, threw himself down on his knees before her, and seized her by both her hands. At that moment the door of the drawing-room was opened, and Mr. Greenmantle appeared within the room.

[75]

Philip Hughes could not get upon his feet quick enough to return the furious anger of the look which was thrown on him. There was a difficulty even in disembarrassing himself of poor Emily's hands; so that she, to her father, seemed to be almost equally a culprit with the young man. She uttered a slight scream, and then he very gradually rose to his legs.

'Emily,' said the angry father, 'retire at once to your chamber.'

'But, papa, I must explain.'

'Retire at once to your chamber, miss. As for this young man, I do not know whether the laws of his country will not punish him for this intrusion.'

Emily was terribly frightened by this allusion to her country's laws. 'He has done nothing, papa; indeed he has done nothing.'

'His very presence here, and on his knees! Is that nothing? Mr. Hughes, I desire that you will retire. Your presence in the bank is required. I lay upon you my strict order never again to presume to come through that door. Where is the servant who announced you?'

'No servant announced me.'

'And did you dare to force your way into my private house, and into my daughter's presence unannounced? It is indeed time that I should take her abroad to undergo a prolonged residence in some foreign parts. But the laws of the country which you have outraged will punish you. In the meantime why do you not withdraw? Am I to be obeyed?'

'I have just one word which I wish to say to Miss Greenmantle.'

'Not a word. Withdraw! I tell you, sir, withdraw to the bank. There your presence is required. Here it will never be needed.'

'Good-bye, Emily,' he said, putting out his hand in his vain attempt to take hers.

'Withdraw, I tell you.' And Mr. Greenmantle, with all the stiffness of the poker apparent about him, backed poor young Philip Hughes through the doorway on to the staircase, and then banged the door behind him. Having done this, he threw himself on to the sofa, and hid his face with his hands. He wished it to be understood that the honour of his family had been altogether disgraced by the lightness of his daughter's conduct.

But his daughter did not see the matter quite in the same light. Though she lacked something of that firmness of manner which Polly Peppercorn was prepared to exhibit, she did not intend to be altogether trodden on. 'Papa,' she said, 'why do you do that?'

'Good heavens!'

'Why do you cover up your face?'

'That a daughter of mine should have behaved so disgracefully!'

'I haven't behaved disgracefully, papa.'

'Admitting a young man surreptitiously to my drawing-room!'

'I didn't admit him; he walked in.'

'And on his knees! I found him on his knees.'

'I didn't put him there. Of course he came,—because,—because—'

'Because what?' he demanded.

'Because he is my lover. I didn't tell him to come; but of course he wanted to see me before we went away.'

'He shall see you no more.'

'Why shouldn't he see me? He's a very good young man, and I am very fond of him. That's just the truth.'

'You shall be taken away for a prolonged residence in foreign parts before another week has passed over your head.'

'Dr. Freeborn quite approves of Mr. Hughes,' pleaded Emily. But the plea at the present moment was of no avail. Mr. Greenmantle in his present frame of mind was almost as angry with Dr. Freeborn as with Emily or Philip Hughes. Dr. Freeborn was joined in this frightful conspiracy against him.

'I do not know,' said he grandiloquently, 'that Dr. Freeborn has any right to interfere with the private affairs of my family. Dr. Freeborn is simply the Rector of Plumplington,—nothing more.'

'He wants to see the people around him all happy,' said Emily.

'He won't see me happy,' said Mr. Greenmantle with awful pride.

'He always wishes to have family quarrels settled before Christmas.'

'He shan't settle anything for me.' Mr. Greenmantle, as he so expressed himself, determined to

maintain his own independence. 'Why is he to interfere with my family quarrels because he's the Rector
of Plumplington? I never heard of such a thing. When
I shall have taken up my residence in foreign parts he
will have no right to interfere with me.'

'But, papa, he will be my clergyman all the same.'

'He won't be mine, I can tell him that. And as for
settling things by Christmas, it is all nonsense. Christmas, except for going to church and taking the Sacra-
ment, is no more than any other day.'

'Oh papa!'

'Well, my dear, I don't quite mean that. What I do
mean is that Dr. Freeborn has no more right to interfere with my family at this time of the year than at
any other. And when you're abroad, which you will
be before Christmas, you'll find that Dr. Freeborn will
have nothing to say to you there.' 'You had better
begin to pack up at once,' he said on the following day.

'Pack up?'

'Yes, pack up. I shall take you first to London,
where you will stay for a day or two. You will go by
the afternoon train to-morrow.'

'To-morrow!'

'I will write and order beds to-day.'

'But where are we to go?'

'That will be made known to you in due time,' said
Mr. Greenmantle.

'But I've got no clothes,' said Emily.

'France is a land in which ladies delight to buy their
dresses.'

'But I shall want all manner of things,—boots and underclothing,—and—and linen, papa.'

'They have all those things in France.'

'But they won't fit me. I always have my things made to fit me. And I haven't got any boxes.'

'Boxes! what boxes? work-boxes?'

'To put my things in. I can't pack up unless I've got something to pack them in. As to going to-morrow, papa, it's quite impossible. Of course there are people I must say good-bye to. The Freeborns—'

'Not the slightest necessity,' said Mr. Greenmantle. 'Dr. Freeborn will quite understand the reason. As to boxes, you won't want the boxes till you've bought the things to put in them.'

'But, papa, I can't go without taking a quantity of things with me. I can't get everything new; and then I must have my dresses made to fit me.' She was very lachrymose, very piteous, and full of entreaties; but still she knew what she was about. As the result of the interview, Mr. Greenmantle did almost acknowledge that they could not depart for a prolonged residence abroad on the morrow.

Early on the following morning Polly Peppercorn came to call. For the last month she had stuck to her resolution,—that she and Miss Greenmantle belonged to different sets in society, and could not be brought together, as Polly had determined to wear her second-rate dresses in preparation for a second-rate marriage,—and this visit was supposed to be something altogether out of the way. It was clearly a visit with a cause, as it was made at eleven o'clock in the morning. 'Oh, Miss Greenmantle,' she said, 'I hear that you're going away to France,—you and your papa, quite at once.'

'Who has told you?'

'Well, I can't quite say; but it has come round through Dr. Freeborn.' Dr. Freeborn had in truth told Mr. Peppercorn, with the express view of exercising what influence he possessed so as to prevent the rapid emigration of Mr. Greenmantle. And Mr. Peppercorn had told his daughter, threatening her that something of the same kind would have to happen in his own family if she proved obstinate about her lover. 'It's the best thing going,' said Mr. Peppercorn, 'when a girl is upsetting and determined to have her own way.' To this Polly made no reply, but came away early on the following morning, so as to converse with her late friend, Miss Greenmantle.

'Papa says so; but you know it's quite impossible.'

'What is Mr. Hughes to do?' asked Polly in a whisper.

'I don't know what anybody is to do. It's dreadful, the idea of going away from home in this sudden manner.'

'Indeed it is.'

'I can't do it. Only think, Polly, when I talk to him about clothes he tells me I'm to buy dresses in some foreign town. He knows nothing about a woman's clothes;—nor yet a man's for the matter of that. Fancy starting to-morrow for six months. It's the sort of thing that Ida Pfeiffer used to do.'

'I didn't know her,' said Polly.

[81]

'She was a great traveller, and went about everywhere almost without anything. I don't know how she managed it, but I'm sure that I can't.'

'Dr. Freeborn says that he thinks it's all nonsense.' As Polly said this she shook her head and looked uncommonly wise. Emily, however, made no immediate answer. Could it be true that Dr. Freeborn had thus spoken of her father? Emily did think that it was all nonsense, but she had not yet brought herself to express her thoughts openly. 'To tell the truth, Miss Greenmantle,' continued Polly, 'Dr. Freeborn thinks that Mr. Hughes ought to be allowed to have his own way.' In answer to this Emily could bring herself to say nothing; but she declared to herself that since the beginning of things Dr. Freeborn had always been as near an angel as any old gentleman could be. 'And he says that it's quite out of the question that you should be carried off in this way.'

'I suppose I must do what papa tells me.'

'Well; yes. I don't know quite about that. I'm all for doing everything that papa likes, but when he talks of taking me to France, I know I'm not going. Lord love you, he couldn't talk to anybody there.' Emily began to remember that her father's proficiency in the French language was not very great. 'Neither could I for the matter of that,' continued Polly. 'Of course, I learned it at school, but when one can only read words very slowly one can't talk them at all. I've tried it, and I know it. A precious figure father and I would make finding our way about France.'

'Does Mr. Peppercorn think of going?' asked Emily.

'He says so;–if I won't drop Jack Hollycombe. Now I don't mean to drop Jack Hollycombe; not for father nor for anyone. It's only Jack himself can make me do that.'

'He won't, I suppose.'

'I don't think he will. Now it's absurd, you know, the idea of our papas both carrying us off to France because we've got lovers in Plumplington. How all the world would laugh at them! You tell your papa what my papa is saying, and Dr. Freeborn thinks that that will prevent him. At any rate, if I were you, I wouldn't go and buy anything in a hurry. Of course, you've got to think of what would do for married life.'

'Oh, dear, no!' exclaimed Emily.

'At any rate I should keep my mind fixed upon it. Dr. Freeborn says that there's no knowing how things may turn out.' Having finished the purport of her embassy, Polly took her leave without even having offered one kiss to her friend.

Dr. Freeborn had certainly been very sly in instigating Mr. Peppercorn to proclaim his intention of following the example of his neighbour the banker. 'Papa,' said Emily when her father came in to luncheon, 'Mr. Peppercorn is going to take his daughter to foreign parts.'

'What for?'

'I believe he means to reside there for a time.'

'What nonsense! He reside in France! He wouldn't know what to do with himself for an hour. I never

[83]

heard anything like it. Because I am going to France is all Plumplington to follow me? What is Mr. Peppercorn's reason for going to France?' Emily hesitated; but Mr. Greenmantle pressed the question, 'What object can such a man have?'

'I suppose it's about his daughter,' said Emily. Then the truth flashed upon Mr. Greenmantle's mind, and he became aware that he must at any rate for the present abandon the idea. Then, too, there came across him some vague notion that Dr. Freeborn had instigated Mr. Peppercorn and an idea of the object with which he had done so.

'Papa,' said Emily that afternoon, 'am I to get the trunks I spoke about?'

'What trunks?'

'To put my things in, papa. I must have trunks if I am to go abroad for any length of time. And you will want a large portmanteau. You would get it much better in London than you would at Plumplington.' But here Mr. Greenmantle told his daughter that she need not at present trouble her mind about either his travelling gear or her own.

A few days afterwards Dr. Freeborn sauntered into the bank, and spoke a few words to the cashier across the counter. 'So Mr. Greenmantle, I'm told, is not going abroad,' said the Rector.

'I've heard nothing more about it,' said Philip Hughes.

'I think he has abandoned the idea. There was Hickory Peppercorn thinking of going, too, but he has abandoned it. What do they want to go travelling about France for?'

'What indeed, Dr. Freeborn;—unless the two young ladies have something to say to it.'

'I don't think they wish it, if you mean that.'

'I think their fathers thought of taking them out of harm's way.'

'No doubt. But when the harm's way consists of a lover it's very hard to tear a young lady away from it.' This was said so that Philip only could hear it. The two lads who attended the bank were away at their desks in distant parts of the office. 'Do you keep your eyes open, Philip,' said the Rector, 'and things will run smoother yet than you expected.'

'He is frightfully angry with me, Dr. Freeborn. I made my way up into the drawing-room the other day, and he found me there.'

'What business had you to do that?'

'Well, I was wrong, I suppose. But if Emily was to be taken away suddenly I had to see her before she went. Think, Doctor, what a prolonged residence in a foreign country means. I mightn't see her again for years.'

'And so he found you up in the drawing-room. It was very improper; that's all I can say. Nevertheless, if you'll behave yourself, I shouldn't be surprised if things were to run smoother before Christmas.' Then the Doctor took his leave.

'Now, father,' said Polly, 'you're not going to carry me off to foreign parts.'

[85]

'Yes, I am. As you're so wilful it's the only thing for you.'

'What's to become of the brewery?'

'The brewery may take care of itself. As you won't want the money for your husband there'll be plenty for me. I'll give it up. I ain't going to slave and slave all my life and nothing come of it. If you won't oblige me in this the brewery may go and take care of itself.'

'If you're like that, father, I must take care of myself. Mr. Greenmantle isn't going to take his daughter over.'

'Yes; he is.'

'Not a bit of it. He's as much as told Emily that she's not to get her things ready.' Then there was a pause, during which Mr. Peppercorn showed that he was much disturbed. 'Now, father, why don't you give way, and show yourself what you always were,–the kindest father that ever a girl had.'

'There's no kindness in you, Polly. Kindness ought to be reciprocal.'

'Isn't it natural that a girl should like her young man?'

'He's not your young man.'

'He's going to be. What have you got to say against him? You ask Dr. Freeborn.'

'Dr. Freeborn, indeed! He isn't your father!'

'He's not my father, but he's my friend. And he's yours, if you only knew it. You think of it, just for another day, and then say that you'll be good to your girl.' Then she kissed him, and as she left him she felt that she was about to prevail.

[86]

CHAPTER SEVEN

THE YOUNG LADIES ARE TO REMAIN AT HOME

MISS Emily Greenmantle had always possessed a certain character for delicacy. We do not mean delicacy of sentiment. That of course belonged to her as a young lady,–but delicacy of health. She was not strong and robust, as her friend Polly Peppercorn. When we say that she possessed that character, we intend to imply that she perhaps made a little use of it. There had never been much the matter with her, but she had always been a little delicate. It seemed to suit her, and prevented the necessity of over-exertion. Whereas Polly, who had never been delicate, felt herself always called upon to 'run round,' as the Americans say. 'Running round' on the part of a young lady implies a readiness and a willingness to do everything that has to be done in domestic life. If a father wants his slippers or a mother her thimble, or the cook a further supply of sauces, the active young lady has to 'run round.' Polly did run round; but Emily was delicate and did not. Therefore when she did not get up one morning, and complained of a headache, the doctor was sent for. 'She's not very strong, you know,' the doctor said to her father. 'Miss Emily always was delicate.'

'I hope it isn't much,' said Mr. Greenmantle.

'There is something I fear disturbing the even tenor

of her thoughts,' said the doctor, who had probably heard of the hopes entertained by Mr. Philip Hughes and favoured them. 'She should be kept quite quiet. I wouldn't prescribe much medicine, but I'll tell Mixet to send her in a little draught. As for diet she can have pretty nearly what she pleases. She never had a great appetite.' And so the doctor went his way. The reader is not to suppose that Emily Greenmantle intended to deceive her father, and play the old soldier. Such an idea would have been repugnant to her nature. But when her father told her that she was to be taken abroad for a prolonged residence, and when it of course followed that her lover was to be left behind, there came upon her a natural feeling that the best thing for her would be to lie in bed, and so to avoid all the troubles of life for the present moment.

'I am very sorry to hear that Emily is so ill,' said Dr. Freeborn, calling on the banker further on in the day.

'I don't think it's much, Dr. Freeborn.'

'I hope not; but I just saw Miller, who shook his head. Miller never shakes his head quite for nothing.'

In the evening Mr. Greenmantle got a little note from Mrs. Freeborn. 'I am *so unhappy* to hear about *dear* Emily. The poor child always is *delicate*. *Pray* take care of her. She must see Dr. Miller twice every day. Changes do take place so *frequently*. If you think she would be better here, we would be *delighted* to have her. There is so much in having the attention of a *lady*.'

'Of course I am nervous,' said Mr. Philip Hughes next morning to the banker. 'I hope you will excuse

[88]

'Then I shall go to bed,' said Polly, 'and send for Dr. Miller to-morrow. I don't see why I'm not to have the same advantage as other girls. But, father, I wouldn't make you unhappy, and I wouldn't cost you a shilling I could help, and I wouldn't not wait upon you for anything. I wouldn't pretend to be ill,—not for Jack Hollycombe.'

'I should find you out if you did.'

'I wouldn't fight my battle except on the square for any earthly consideration. But, father—'

'What do you want of me?'

'I am broken-hearted about him. Though I look red in the face, and fat, and all that, I suffer quite as much as Emily Greenmantle. When I tell him to wait perhaps for years, I know I'm unreasonable. When a young man wants a wife, he wants one. He has made up his mind to settle down, and he doesn't expect a girl to bid him remain as he is for another four or five years.'

'You've no business to tell him anything of the kind.'

'When he asks me I have a business,—if it's true. Father!'

'Well!'

'It is true. I don't know whether it ought to be so, but it is true. I'm very fond of you.'

'You don't show it.'

'Yes, I am. And I think I do show it, for I do whatever you tell me. But I like him the best.'

'What has he done for you?'

[91]

'Nothing;—not half so much as I have done for him. But I do like him the best. It's human nature. I don't take on to tell him so;—only once. Once I told him that I loved him better than all the rest,—and that if he chose to take my word for it, once spoken, he might have it. He did choose, and I'm not going to repeat it, till I tell him when I can be his own.'

'He'll have to take you just as you stand.'

'May be; but it will be worth while for him to wait just a little, till he shall see what you mean to do. What do you mean to do with it, father? We don't want it at once.'

'He's not edicated as a gentleman should be.'

'Are you?'

'No; but I didn't try to get a young woman with money. I made the money, and I've a right to choose the sort of son-in-law my daughter shall marry.'

'No; never!' she said.

'Then he must take you just as you are; and I'll make ducks and drakes of the money after my own fashion. If you were married to-morrow what do you mean to live upon?'

'Forty shillings a week. I've got it all down in black and white.'

'And when children come;—one after another, year by year.'

'Do as others do. I'll go bail my children won't starve;—or his. I'd work for them down to my bare bones. But would you look on the while, making ducks and drakes of your money, or spending it at the

[92]

pot-house, just to break the heart of your own child? It's not in you to do it. You'd have to alter your nature first. You speak of yourself as though you were strong as iron. There isn't a bit of iron about you; – but there's something a deal better. You are one of those men, father, who are troubled with a heart.'

'You're one of those women,' said he, 'who trouble the world by their tongues.' Then he bounced out of the house and banged the door.

He had seen Jack Hollycombe through the window going down to the brewery, and he now slowly followed the young man's steps. He went very slowly as he got to the entrance to the brewery yard, and there he paused for a while thinking over the condition of things. 'Hang the fellow,' he said to himself; 'what on earth has he done that he should have it all his own way. I never had it all my way. I had to work for it; – and precious hard too. My wife had to cook the dinner with only just a slip of a girl to help make the bed. If he'd been a gentleman there'd have been something in it. A gentleman expects to have things ready to his hand. But he's to walk into all my money just because he's good-looking. And then Polly tells me, that I can't help myself because I'm good-natured. I'll let her know whether I'm good-natured! If he wants a wife he must support a wife; – and he shall.' But though Mr. Peppercorn stood in the doorway murmuring after this fashion he knew very well that he was about to lose the battle. He had come down the street on purpose to signify to Jack Hollycombe that he might go up and settle the day with Polly; and he himself in the midst of all his objurgations was picturing to himself the delight with which he would see Polly restored to her former mode of dressing. 'Well, Mr. Hollycombe, are you here?'

'Yes, Mr. Peppercorn, I am here.'

'So I perceive,—as large as life. I don't know what on earth you're doing over here so often. You're wasting your employers' time, I believe.'

'I came over to see Messrs. Grist and Grindall's young man.'

'I don't believe you came to see any young man at all.'

'It wasn't any young woman, as I haven't been to your house, Mr. Peppercorn.'

'What's the good of going to my house? There isn't any young woman there can do you any good.' Then Mr. Peppercorn looked round and saw that there were others within hearing to whom the conversation might be attractive. 'Do you come in here. I've got something to say to you.' Then he led the way into his own little parlour, and shut the door. 'Now Mr. Hollycombe, I've got something to communicate.'

'Out with it, Mr. Peppercorn.'

'There's that girl of mine up there is the biggest fool that ever was since the world began.'

'It's astonishing,' said Jack, 'what different opinions different people have about the same thing.'

'I daresay. That's all very well for you; but I say she's a fool. What on earth can she see in you to make her want to give you all my money?'

'She can't do that unless you're so pleased.'

'And she won't neither. If you like to take her, there she is.'

'Mr. Peppercorn, you make me the happiest man in the world.'

'I don't make you the richest;—and you're going to make yourself about the poorest. To marry a wife upon forty shillings a week! I did it myself, however,—upon thirty-five, and I hadn't any stupid old father-in-law to help me out. I'm not going to see her break her heart; and so you may go and tell her. But you needn't tell her as I'm going to make her any regular allowance. Only tell her to put on some decent kind of gown, before I come home to tea. Since all this came up the slut has worn the same dress she bought three winters ago. She thinks I didn't know it.'

And so Mr. Peppercorn had given way; and Polly was to be allowed to flaunt it again this Christmas in silks and satins. 'Now you'll give me a kiss,' said Jack when he had told his tale.

'I've only got it on your bare word,' she answered, turning away from him.

'Why; he sent me here himself; and says you're to put on a proper frock to give him his tea in.'

'No.'

'But he did.'

'Then, Jack, you shall have a kiss. I am sure the message about the frock must have come from himself. Jack, are you not the happiest young man in all Plumplington?'

'How about the happiest young woman,' said Jack.

'Well, I don't mind owning up. I am. But it's for your sake. I could have waited, and not have been a bit impatient. But it's so different with a man. Did he say, Jack, what he meant to do for you?'

'He swore that he would not give us a penny.'

'But that's rubbish. I am not going to let you marry till I know what's fixed. Nor yet will I put on my silk frock.'

'You must. He'll be sure to go back if you don't do that. I should risk it all now, if I were you.'

'And so make a beggar of you. My husband shall not be dependent on any man,—not even on father. I shall keep my clothes on as I've got 'em till something is settled.'

'I wouldn't anger him if I were you,' said Jack cautiously.

'One has got to anger him sometimes, and all for his own good. There's the frock hanging up-stairs, and I'm as fond of a bit of finery as any girl. Well;—I'll put it on to-night because he has made something of a promise; but I'll not continue it till I know what he means to do for you. When I'm married my husband will have to pay for my clothes, and not father.'

'I guess you'll pay for them yourself.'

'No, I shan't. It's not the way of the world in this part of England. One of you must do it, and I won't have it done by father,—not regular. As I begin so I must go on. Let him tell me what he means to do and then we shall know how we're to live. I'm not a bit afraid of you and your forty shillings.'

'My girl!' Here was some little attempt at embracing, which, however, Polly checked.

'There's no good in all that when we're talking business. I look upon it now that we're to be married as soon as I please. Father has given way as to that, and I don't want to put you off.'

'Why no! You ought not to do that when you think what I have had to endure.'

'If you had known the picture which father drew just now of what we should have to suffer on your forty shillings a week!'

'What did he say, Polly?'

'Never mind what he said. Dry bread would be the best of it. I don't care about the dry bread;—but if there is to be anything better it must be all fixed. You must have the money for your own.'

'I don't suppose he'll do that.'

'Then you must take me without the money. I'm not going to have him giving you a five-pound note at the time and your having to ask for it. Nor yet am I going to ask for it. I don't mind it now. And to give him his due, I never asked him for a sovereign but what he gave me two. He's very generous.'

'Is he now?'

'But he likes to have the opportunity. I won't live in the want of any man's generosity,—only my husband's. If he chooses to do anything extra that'll be as he likes it. But what we have to live upon,—to pay for meat and coals and such like,—that must be your own. I'll put on the dress to-night because I won't vex

[97]

G

him. But before he goes to bed he must be made to understand all that. And you must understand it too, Jack. As we mean to go on so must we begin!' The interview ended, however, in an invitation given to Jack to stay in Plumplington and eat his supper. He knew the road so well that he could drive himself home in the dark.

'I suppose I'd better let them have two hundred a year to begin with,' said Peppercorn to himself, sitting alone in his little parlour. 'But I'll keep it in my own hands. I'm not going to trust that fellow further than I can see him.'

But on this point he had to change his mind before he went to bed. He was gracious enough to Jack as they were eating their supper, and insisted on having a hot glass of brandy and water afterwards,—all in honour of Polly's altered dress. But as soon as Jack was gone Polly explained her views of the case, and spoke such undoubted wisdom as she sat on her father's knee, that he was forced to yield. 'I'll speak to Mr. Scribble about having it all properly settled.' Now Mr. Scribble was the Plumplington attorney.

'Two hundred a year, father, which is to be Jack's own,—for ever. I won't marry him for less,—not to live as you propose.'

'When I say a thing I mean it,' said Peppercorn. Then Polly retired, having given him a final kiss.

About a fortnight after this Mr. Greenmantle came to the Rectory and desired to see Dr. Freeborn. Since Emily had been taken ill there had not been many signs of friendship between the Greenmantle and the Freeborn houses. But now there he was in the Rectory hall, and within five minutes had followed the Rectory footman into Dr. Freeborn's study. 'Well, Greenmantle, I'm delighted to see you. How's Emily?'

Mr. Greenmantle might have been delighted to see the Doctor but he didn't look it. 'I trust that she is somewhat better. She has risen from her bed to-day.'

'I'm glad to hear that,' said the Doctor.

'Yes; she got up yesterday, and to-day she seems to be restored to her usual health.'

'That's good news. You should be careful with her and not let her trust too much to her strength. Miller said that she was very weak, you know.'

'Yes; Miller has said so all through,' said the father; 'but I'm not quite sure that Miller has understood the case.'

'He hasn't known all the ins and outs you mean,— about Philip Hughes.' Here the Doctor smiled, but Mr. Greenmantle moved about uneasily as though the poker were at work. 'I suppose Philip Hughes had something to do with her malady.'

'The truth is—,' began Mr. Greenmantle.

'What's the truth?' asked the Doctor. But Mr. Greenmantle looked as though he could not tell his tale without many efforts. 'You heard what old Peppercorn has done with his daughter?—Settled £250 a year on her for ever, and has come to me asking me whether I can't marry them on Christmas Day. Why if they were to be married by banns there would not be time.'

'I don't see why they shouldn't be married by banns,' said Mr. Greenmantle, who amidst all these difficulties disliked nothing so much as that he should be put into the category with Mr. Peppercorn, or Emily with Polly Peppercorn.

'I say nothing about that. I wish everybody was married by banns. Why shouldn't they? But that's not to be. Polly came to me the next day, and said that her father didn't know what he was talking about.'

'I suppose she expects a special licence like the rest of them,' said Mr. Greenmantle.

'What the girls think mostly of is their clothes. Polly wouldn't mind the banns the least in the world; but she says she can't have her things ready. When a young lady talks about her things a man has to give up. Polly says that February is a very good month to be married in.'

Mr. Greenmantle was again annoyed, and showed it by the knitting of his brow, and the increased stiffness of his head and shoulders. The truth may as well be told. Emily's illness had prevailed with him and he too had yielded. When she had absolutely refused to look at her chicken-broth for three consecutive days her father's heart had been stirred. For Mr. Green-mantle's character will not have been adequately described unless it be explained that the stiffness lay rather in the neck and shoulders than in the organism by which his feelings were conducted. He was in truth very like Mr. Peppercorn, though he would have been infuriated had he been told so. When he found himself alone after his defeat,—which took place at once when the chicken-broth had gone down untasted for the third time,—he was ungainly and ill-natured to look at. But he went to work at once to make excuses for Philip Hughes, and ended by assuring himself that he was a manly honest sort of fellow, who was sure to do well in his profession; and ended by assuring himself that it would be very comfortable to have his married daughter and her husband living with him. He at once saw Philip, and explained to him that he had certainly done very wrong in coming up to his drawing-room without leave. 'There is an etiquette in those things which no doubt you will learn as you grow older.' Philip thought that the etiquette wouldn't much matter as soon as he had married his wife. And he was wise enough to do no more than beg Mr. Greenmantle's pardon for the fault which he had committed. 'But as I am informed by my daughter,' continued Mr. Greenmantle, 'that her affections are irrevocably settled upon you,'—here Philip could only bow,—'I am prepared to withdraw my opposition, which has only been entertained as long as I thought it necessary for my daughter's happiness. There need be no words now,' he continued, seeing that Philip was about to speak, 'but when I shall have made up my mind as to what it may be fitting that I shall do in regard to money, then I will see you again. In the meantime you're welcome to come into my drawing-room when it may suit you to pay your respects to Miss Greenmantle.' It was speedily settled that the marriage should take place in February, and Mr. Greenmantle was now informed that Polly Peppercorn and Mr. Hollycombe were to be married in the same month!

He had resolved, however, after much consideration, that he would himself inform Dr. Freeborn that he had given way, and had now come for this purpose. There would be less of triumph to the enemy, and less of disgrace to himself, if he were to declare the truth. And there no longer existed any possibility of a permanent quarrel with the Doctor. The prolonged residence abroad had altogether gone to the winds. 'I think I will just step over and tell the Doctor of this alteration in our plans.' This he had said to Emily, and Emily had thanked him and kissed him, and once again had called him 'her own dear papa.' He had suffered greatly during the period of his embittered feelings, and now had his reward. For it is not to be supposed that when a man has swallowed a poker the evil results will fall only upon his companions. The process is painful also to himself. He cannot breathe in comfort so long as the poker is there.

'And so Emily too is to have her lover. I am delighted to hear it. Believe me she hasn't chosen badly. Philip Hughes is an excellent young fellow. And so we shall have the double marriage coming after all.' Here the poker was very visible. 'My wife will go and see her at once, and congratulate her; and so will I as soon as I have heard that she's got herself properly dressed for drawing-room visitors. Of course I may congratulate Philip.'

[102]

'Yes, you may do that,' said Mr. Greenmantle very stiffly.

'All the town will know all about it before it goes to bed to-night. It is better so. There should never be a mystery about such matters. Good-bye, Greenmantle, I congratulate you with all my heart.'

CHAPTER EIGHT

CHRISTMAS-DAY

'NOW I'll tell you what we'll do,' said the Doctor to his wife a few days after the two marriages had been arranged in the manner thus described. It yet wanted ten days to Christmas, and it was known to all Plumplington that the Doctor intended to be more than ordinarily blithe during the present Christmas holidays. 'We'll have these young people to dinner on Christmas-day, and their fathers shall come with them.'

'Will that do, Doctor,?' said his wife

'Why should it not do?'

'I don't think that Mr. Greenmantle will care about meeting Mr. Peppercorn.'

'If Mr. Peppercorn dines at my table,' said the Doctor with a certain amount of arrogance, 'any gentleman in England may meet him. What! not meet a fellow townsman on Christmas-day and on such an occasion as this!'

'I don't think he'll like it,' said Mrs. Freeborn.

'Then he may lump it. You'll see he'll come. He'll not like to refuse to bring Emily here, especially as she is to meet her betrothed. And the Peppercorns and Jack Hollycombe will be sure to come. Those sort of vagaries as to meeting this man and not that, in sitting next to one woman and objecting to another, don't prevail on Christmas-day, thank God. They've met already at the Lord's Supper, or ought to have met;

and they surely can meet afterwards at the parson's table. And we'll have Harry Gresham to show that there is no ill-will. I hear that Harry is already making up to the Dean's daughter at Barchester.'

'He won't care whom he meets,' said Mrs. Freeborn. 'He has got a position of his own and can afford to meet anybody. It isn't quite so with Mr. Greenmantle. But of course you can have it as you please. I shall be delighted to have Polly and her husband at dinner with us.'

So it was settled and the invitations were sent out. That to the Peppercorns was despatched first, so that Mr. Greenmantle might be informed whom he would have to meet. It was conveyed in a note from Mrs. Freeborn to Polly, and came in the shape of an order rather than of a request. 'Dr. Freeborn hopes that your Papa and Mr. Hollycombe will bring you to dine with us on Christmas-day at six o'clock. We'll try and get Emily Greenmantle and her lover to meet you. You must come because the Doctor has set his heart upon it.'

'That's very civil,' said Mr. Peppercorn. 'Shan't I get any dinner till six o'clock?'

'You can have lunch, father, of course. You must go.'

'A bit of bread and cheese when I come out of church – just when I'm most famished! Of course I'll go. I never dined with the Doctor before.'

'Nor did I; but I've drunk tea there. You'll find he'll make himself very pleasant. But what are we to do about Jack.'

'He'll come of course.'

'But what are we to do about his clothes?' said Polly. 'I don't think he's got a dress coat; and I'm sure he hasn't a white tie. Let him come just as he pleases, they won't mind on Christmas-day as long as he's clean. He'd better come over and go to church with us; and then I'll see as to making him up tidy.' Word was sent to say that Polly and her father and her lover would come, and the necessary order was at once despatched to Barchester.

'I really do not know what to say about it,' said Mr. Greenmantle when the invitation was read to him. 'You will meet Polly Peppercorn and her husband as is to be,' Mrs. Freeborn had written in her note; 'for we look on you and Polly as the two heroines of Plumplington for this occasion.' Mr. Greenmantle had been struck with dismay as he read the words. Could he bring himself to sit down to dinner with Hickory Peppercorn and Jack Hollycombe; and ought he to do so? Or could he refuse the Doctor's invitation on such an occasion? He suggested at first that a letter should be prepared declaring that he did not like to take his Christmas dinner away from his own house. But to this Emily would by no means consent. She had plucked up her spirits greatly since the days of the chicken-broth, and was determined at the present moment to rule both her future husband and her father. 'You must go, papa. I wouldn't not go for all the world.'

'I don't see it, my dear; indeed I don't.'

'The Doctor has been so kind. What's your objection, papa?'

'There are differences, my dear.'

'But Dr. Freeborn likes to have them.'

'A clergyman is very peculiar. The rector of a parish can always meet his own flock. But rank is rank you know, and it behoves me to be careful with whom I shall associate. I shall have Mr. Peppercorn slapping my back and poking me in the ribs some of these days. And moreover they have joined your name with that of the young lady in a manner that I do not quite approve. Though you each of you may be a heroine in your own way, you are not the two heroines of Plumplington. I do not choose that you shall appear together in that light.'

'That is only his joke,' said Emily.

'It is a joke to which I do not wish to be a party. The two heroines of Plumplington! It sounds like a vulgar farce.'

Then there was a pause, during which Mr. Greenmantle was thinking how to frame the letter of excuse by which he would avoid the difficulty. But at last Emily said a word which settled him. 'Oh, papa, they'll say that you were too proud, and then they'll laugh at you.' Mr. Greenmantle looked very angry at this, and was preparing himself to use some severe language to his daughter. But he remembered how recently she had become engaged to be married, and he abstained. 'As you wish it, we will go,' he said. 'At the present crisis of your life I would not desire to disappoint you in anything.' So it happened that the Doctor's proposed guests all accepted; for Harry Gresham too expressed himself as quite delighted to meet Emily Greenmantle on the auspicious occasion.

'I shall be delighted also to meet Jack Hollycombe,' Harry had said. 'I have known him ever so long and have just given him an order for twenty quarters of oats.'

They were all to be seen at the Parish Church of Plumplington on that Christmas morning;—except Harry Gresham, who, if he did so at all, went to church at Greshamsbury,—and the Plumplington world all looked at them with admiring eyes. As it happened the Peppercorns sat just behind the Greenmantles, and on this occasion Jack Hollycombe and Polly were exactly in the rear of Philip Hughes and Emily. Mr. Greenmantle as he took his seat observed that it was so, and his devotions were, we fear, disturbed by the fact. He walked up proudly to the altar among the earliest and most aristocratic recipients, and as he did so could not keep himself from turning round to see whether Hickory Peppercorn was treading on his kibes. But on the present occasion Hickory Peppercorn was very modest and remained with his future son-in-law nearly to the last.

At six o'clock they all met in the Rectory drawing-room. 'Our two heroines,' said the Doctor as they walked in, one just after the other, each leaning on her lover's arm. Mr. Greenmantle looked as though he did not like it. In truth he was displeased, but he could not help himself. Of the two young ladies Polly was by far the most self-possessed. As long as she had got the husband of her choice she did not care whether she were or were not called a heroine. And her father had behaved very well on that morning as to money. 'If you come out like that, father,' she had said, 'I shall have to wear a silk dress every day.' 'So you ought,' he said with true Christmas generosity. But the income then promised had been a solid assurance, and Polly was the best contented young woman in all Plumplington.

They all sat down to dinner, the Doctor with a bride on each side of him, the place of honour to his right having been of course accorded to Emily Greenmantle; and next to each young lady was her lover. Miss Greenmantle as was her nature was very quiet, but Philip Hughes made an effort and carried on, as best he could, a conversation with the Doctor. Jack Holly-combe till after pudding-time said not a word and Polly tried to console herself through his silence by remembering that the happiness of the world did not depend upon loquacity. She herself said a little word now and again, always with a slight effort to bring Jack into notice. But the Doctor with his keen power of observation understood them all, and told himself that Jack was to be a happy man. At the other end of the table Mr. Greenmantle and Mr. Peppercorn sat opposite to each other, and they too, till after pudding-time, were very quiet. Mr. Peppercorn felt himself to be placed a little above his proper position, and could not at once throw off the burden. And Mr. Greenmantle would not make the attempt. He felt that an injury had been done him in that he had been made to sit opposite to Hickory Peppercorn. And in truth the dinner party as a dinner party would have been a failure, had it not been for Harry Gresham, who, seated in the middle between Philip and Mr. Peppercorn, felt it incumbent upon him in his present position to keep up the rattle of the conversation. He said a good deal about the 'two heroines,' and the two heroes, till Polly felt herself bound to quiet him by saying that it was a pity that there was not another heroine also for him.

'I'm an unfortunate fellow,' said Harry, 'and am always left out in the cold. But perhaps I may be a hero too some of these days.'

Then when the cloth had been removed,–for the Doctor always had the cloth taken off his table,–the jollity of the evening really began. The Doctor delighted to be on his legs on such an occasion and to make a little speech. He said that he had on his right and on his left two young ladies both of whom he had known and had loved throughout their entire lives, and now they were to be delivered over by their fathers, whom he delighted to welcome this Christmas-day at his modest board, each to the man who for the future was to be her lord and her husband. He did not know any occasion on which he, as a pastor of the church, could take greater delight, seeing that in both cases he had ample reason to be satisfied with the choice which the young ladies had made. The bride-grooms were in both instances of such a nature and had made for themselves such characters in the estimation of their friends and neighbours as to give all assurance of the happiness prepared for their wives. There was much more of it, but this was the gist of the Doctor's eloquence. And then he ended by saying that he would ask the two fathers to say a word in acknowledgment of the toast.

This he had done out of affection to Polly, whom he did not wish to distress by calling upon Jack Hollycombe to take a share in the speech-making of the evening. He felt that Jack would require a little practice before he could achieve comfort during such an operation; but the immediate effect was to plunge Mr. Greenmantle into a cold bath. What was he to say on such an opportunity? But he did blunder through, and gave occasion to none of that sorrow which Polly would have felt had Jack Hollycombe got upon his legs, and then been reduced to silence. Mr. Peppercorn in his turn made a better speech than could have been expected from him. He said that he was very proud of his position that day, which was due to his girl's manner and education. He was not entitled to be there by anything that he had done himself. Here the Doctor cried, 'Yes, yes, yes, certainly.' But Peppercorn shook his head. He wasn't specially proud of himself, he said, but he was awfully proud of his girl. And he thought that Jack Hollycombe was about the most fortunate young man of whom he had ever heard. Here Jack declared that he was quite aware of it.

After that the jollity of the evening commenced;

and they were very jolly till the Doctor began to feel that it might be difficult to restrain the spirits which he had raised. But they were broken up before a very late hour by the necessity that Harry Gresham should return to Greshamsbury. Here we must bid farewell to the 'two heroines of Plumplington,' and to their young men, wishing them many joys in their new capacities. One little scene however must be described, which took place as the brides were putting on their hats in the Doctor's study. 'Now I can call you Emily again,' said Polly, 'and now I can kiss you; though I know I ought to do neither the one nor the other.'

'Yes, both, both, always do both,' said Emily. Then Polly walked home with her father, who, however well satisfied he might have been in his heart, had not many words to say on that evening.

The following is a list of other books by Anthony Trollope, in the Harting Grange Library series, published by Caledonia Press.

THE LADY OF LAUNAY

Mrs. Miles, the Lady of Launay, is a widow "possessed of wealth and social position." Martyrly she denies herself all delights, especially the delights of money and society. But what she will not deny herself is her own "idea of duty." For that idea she would turn her son out of her house; and she would force her ward Bessy Pryor to marry a man she cannot love.

ISBN 0-932282-02-4 (softcover)
ISBN 0-932282-03-2 (library binding)

WHY FRAU FROHMANN RAISED HER PRICES

"There you come to people with fixed incomes," said Mr. Cartwright, an Englishman in this novel: "The few who live upon what they have saved or others have saved for them must go to the wall."

This novel, written in 1877, is frankly about inflation and what it does to people.

ISBN 0-932282-05-9 (softcover)
ISBN 0-932282-06-7 (library binding)

CHRISTMAS AT THOMPSON HALL

A Mid-Victorian Christmas tale, in the tradition of Charles Dickens, but with Trollope's unique sense of affection, understanding and humor.

ISBN 0-932282-07-5 (hardcover trade)
ISBN 0-932282-09-1 (library binding)

ALICE DUGDALE

Alice Dugdale is one of Trollope's most intelligent
and modern heroines. The problem is Major Rossiter
doesn't know if he wants a girl intelligent and
strong, or if he prefers one beautiful and fashionable
and dull.

ISBN 0-932282-11-3 (softcover)
ISBN 0-932282-12-1 (library binding)

TWO HEROINES OF PLUMPLINGTON

A Barsetshire Christmas Tale.
Two young girls have given their hearts to young
men their fathers disapprove of. The fathers are
stern, the girls stubborn, and a merry Christmas is
threatened.

ISBN 0-932282-48-2 (softcover)
ISBN 0-932282-49-0 (library binding)

Consult your bookseller for details or write Caledonia
Press for a descriptive catalog.
Caledonia Press
P.O. Box 245
Racine, Wisconsin
52401 U.S.A.